Watch Where You Step. . . .

"Your turn, Nancy," Elsa added, joining George.

Nancy gritted her teeth. She was an experienced rider, but the fence was huge. Still, she was confident that Tristram wouldn't let her down.

Squeezing her legs against the saddle, she urged Tristram into the jump. He shot toward it, his body like an arrow. Nancy hunched forward as the huge animal launched himself into flight. *This is so cool,* she thought as the cornfield streaked up at her.

Tristram's hooves met the ground, and Nancy's eyes widened. A huge hole appeared under his left foot.

D0011632

Nancy Drew
Mystery Stories

Available from Simon & Schuster

NANCY DREW® 172

THE RIDING CLUB CRIME

CAROLYN KEENE

Aladdin Paperbacks
New York   London   Toronto   Sydney   Singapore

If you purchased this book without a cover, you should be aware that this book is stolen property. It was reported as "unsold and destroyed" to the publisher, and neither the author nor the publisher has received any payment for this "stripped book."

This book is a work of fiction. Any references to historical events, real people, or real locales are used fictitiously. Other names, characters, places, and incidents are the product of the author's imagination, and any resemblance to actual events or locales or persons, living or dead, is entirely coincidental.

First Aladdin Paperbacks edition May 2003

Copyright © 2003 by Simon & Schuster, Inc.

ALADDIN PAPERBACKS
An imprint of Simon & Schuster
Children's Publishing Division
1230 Avenue of the Americas
New York, NY 10020

All rights reserved, including the right of
reproduction in whole or in part in any form.

Printed in the United States of America

10 9 8 7 6 5 4 3 2 1

NANCY DREW, NANCY DREW MYSTERY STORIES, and colophon are registered trademarks of Simon & Schuster, Inc.

Library of Congress Control Number 2002115458

ISBN 0-689-86145-1

Contents

1

Green Spring Farm

"Whoa, Tristram!" Nancy Drew said as the horse she was riding leaped into the air. A small gray shape with a furry tail scurried across the path in front of them. "Chill out, boy," she added, "it's only a squirrel."

"I don't know what's gotten into Tristram—he's usually pretty calm," Elsa Gable said. She stopped her horse, Barchester, next to Nancy and scanned the woods. Shafts of sunlight broke through the canopy of leaves above them. "He's been in these woods a million times. Why's he suddenly so scared?"

"Sneak attacks by mutant squirrels," George Fayne said from behind them. "Pretty terrifying, huh, Derby?" She reached down to pat her horse's sleek, golden neck.

1

Nancy and Elsa laughed. "Let's get going," Elsa said, "before any mutants get us."

Elsa was an old friend of Nancy, George, and George's cousin, Bess Marvin. She kept Barchester at Green Spring Farm, a riding stable in the country outside River Heights. She was also a counselor at Green Spring's summer camp, but she had a break while the campers were swimming. George and Nancy had eagerly agreed to ride with her when she'd called to invite them earlier that day.

Nancy led the way down the trail. It quickly brought them to the edge of a meadow. Purple clover and white Queen Anne's lace threaded the long green grass.

"The trail picks up again in the woods across the field," Elsa said. "Want to race?"

Before Nancy had a chance to respond, Barchester sprang into the meadow with Elsa hunched forward in her saddle. His jet-black coat gleamed in the sudden burst of sun. Tristram and Derby bolted after him, tossing their heads and whinnying. Nancy loosened Tristram's reins and nudged him into a gallop.

The breeze slapped against Nancy's face as she and Tristram zoomed through the field, his hooves pounding underneath her. She could hear Barchester and Derby galloping behind. *Are they catching up with me?* she wondered.

Seconds later, she came to the edge of the woods.

"Finish line!" she called, reining Tristram in.

"That was great!" George said, her brown eyes sparkling. She stopped Derby next to Nancy.

"I claim a tie for second!" Elsa said, pulling up by George. She flicked back her long chestnut hair, which had tumbled out from under her helmet.

"No way, Elsa. You're third by a nose," George countered.

Elsa grinned. "Whatever. Anyway, too bad Bess wasn't up for riding with us this afternoon. That would have made for an even better race!"

"Bess was in a race of her own. Her favorite shoe store is having a sale, and she wanted to get to the mall ASAP," George said.

"Maybe she can ride another time," Nancy suggested. "Bess likes horses. It's just that for her, shopping comes first."

Elsa's green eyes looked thoughtful. "Well, since Bess likes both fashion and horses, I might know the perfect job for her: an internship at *The Horse's Mouth*."

Nancy frowned. "*The Horse's Mouth*. That sounds familiar. Is it a magazine?"

"It's a newsletter in River Heights that covers equestrian stuff," Elsa explained. "Anything to do with horses. The editor is a friend of Mrs. Rogers, the owner of Green Spring Farm. She told the counselors to spread the word that the newsletter needs an intern to cover equestrian fashion."

"Bess would love it," Nancy agreed.

"Remind me to call her when we get back to the barn," Elsa said. "In the meantime, we've got a jump at the end of that trail to get over. Nancy, you lead."

Nancy urged Tristram into the woods at a brisk trot. She could hear the other horses following them. When a fork appeared ahead, she tugged on the reins to slow her horse. "Which way, Elsa?"

"We have a choice," Elsa said. "The wimpy log fence to the left, or the giant post-and-rail to the right."

"You call that a choice?" George said, and grinned. "Who wants to be a wimp?"

"Would you be up for jumping it first, George?" Elsa said. "That fence is so big that Barchester always refuses it. But he'll do whatever Derby does. Don't ask me why, but Derby is his role model."

"People have role models, so why shouldn't horses?" Nancy quipped as she guided Tristram to the right. As they walked along single file, she asked Elsa how things were going at the camp. "Are you having fun?" Twisting in her saddle, she studied Elsa's face. Nancy thought she saw Elsa's eyes flicker down before they met her gaze.

"Basically, yeah," Elsa said.

Is Elsa worried about something? Nancy wondered.

4

"Working at a riding camp sounds great," George broke in. "How old are the kids?"

"Fourteen to seventeen," Elsa said. "It's a two-week program, and all the campers are members of the Green Spring Pony Club, which is part of the United States Pony Club. But even though the age limit for Mrs. Rogers's camp is seventeen, you can be in pony club until you're twenty-one. And don't be fooled by the name 'pony club.' Most of the kids actually ride horses."

Nancy thought about the official difference between a pony and a horse. A horse was larger than fourteen and a half hands, while a pony was under that size. Nancy also knew that a hand was the official horse measurement of four inches. But she was curious to know more about the riding club. "How do you get to be a member?" she asked. "Do you have to pass some test?"

Elsa shrugged. "You just apply and pay dues. The camp helps the kids polish their riding skills and get ready for pony club competitions."

"Competitions? Like horse shows and stuff?" George asked.

"Not regular horse shows," Elsa replied. "These are events for pony clubs to compete against one another. For instance, we're getting ready for the pony club rally that starts this Friday. Tomorrow, Mrs. Rogers and all of the counselors will choose five

5

of the most qualified kids to be on Green Spring's rally team."

"What's a pony club rally?" Nancy asked.

"It's a three-day competition between different teams," Elsa explained. "There are regional rallies and national ones. If your team wins the rally in your region, it goes on to compete at the national level. The rally on Friday is a regional one; it's at the Chatham Fairgrounds, about half an hour from River Heights. Six clubs from around the area will be competing."

"What happens during the three days?" George asked.

"Well, this one is a Combined Training Rally, which means it has several events. The first evening we're there, the teams take a written test to quiz their knowledge of horses and riding," Elsa explained. "The next day is dressage. That takes place in a ring bounded by a picket fence about a foot high. Each rider takes his or her horse through a series of circles and figure eights and stuff. The horses have to go at different paces—walking, trotting, and cantering. And the rider has to wear special clothes."

"What kind of clothes?" Nancy asked.

"Basic black. Coat, boots, and derby hat. Oh, and white breeches," Elsa added. "The clothes sound kind of dorky, but the riders actually look pretty cool, especially when their horses have been cleaned and brushed. They're like something out of an old-fashioned movie."

"So the first full day of the rally is just dressage?" Nancy asked.

"Yes, and the second day is cross-country. That's a two-mile course across woods and fields, with about fourteen jumps scattered around. It's awesome. Most of the kids like cross-country best because they're not performing in front of an audience—just the judges who are posted at the jumps."

"What happens on the third day?" George asked.

"Stadium jumping," Elsa told her. "That takes place in a ring in front of the grandstand. The jumps are big, and the officials try to make them look scary and weird, with brightly painted poles and barrels. Sometimes the horses get skittish at the sight of them. If a horse refuses a jump, major penalties are added because the judges think a good rider should be able to make the horse do anything."

"That's unfair," George said. "I mean, horses aren't sheep. A horse has a mind of its own."

"Sure does," Elsa said. "But the rally is judged on the performance of each horse. Whichever team has the best horses and riders will go to the national rally. This year it's in Virginia."

Tristram's reddish brown coat and black mane glistened in the sunlight. Nancy gave him an

T 73176

encouraging pat on his soft neck. "Why only five kids for the team?" Nancy asked, twisting around again to see Elsa. "I bet all the campers are pretty tense about who will make it."

Elsa rolled her eyes. "The competition between them is ridiculous. I wish they'd relax." She sighed. "There are going to be hurt feelings tomorrow, but what can we do? We can't take more than five kids. The teams are the same all over the country: four riders and one stable manager to care for the horses and help the riders."

"Are the rallies fun?" George asked.

Elsa's face lit up. "The rallies are awesome. I guess I can't blame the kids for wanting to go. I just wish they'd appreciate what they're learning at Mrs. Rogers's camp for its own sake and stop worrying about making the team. Her program is really special. I don't know of any other pony club camp like it."

"How's it so special?" Nancy asked as she ducked under a low-hanging branch.

"Mrs. Rogers is a wealthy widow, and she's totally committed to helping kids who can't afford riding camp or keeping horses," Elsa said. "She offers a full scholarship and the use of her own horses to eight girls and boys. They have to be good riders and interested in the sport. The scholarship kids are some of her most serious riders. They make up about a third of the camp, I think."

"So the other kids bring their own horses?" George asked.

"Uh-huh. Mrs. Rogers owns about ten horses, including Tristram and Derby here—not nearly enough horses for all of the campers."

"What a great thing for her to do—use her money to help kids who can't afford her camp," Nancy said.

"Her scholarship is just the beginning of her good deeds," Elsa declared. "She also insists that at least two of the rally team members must be scholarship campers. She's devoted to them, and that's mainly why Green Spring is special. The other reason is Mrs. Rogers's personality."

"What's she like?" George asked.

"Maybe you guys can meet her when we get back to the barn," Elsa said. "She was busy giving lessons earlier. Anyway, she's really friendly and always in a good mood. She has a knack for making kids excited about riding. She also has tons of cool animals in her house—dogs, cats, ferrets, and even a monkey! She lives in this huge Victorian mansion with lots of rooms. Campers stay there instead of in cabins or tents."

"Sounds like camp heaven," George said. "I wish I could go—don't you, Nancy?"

"Too bad we're past the cutoff age!" Nancy said.

The trail widened, and the trees thinned. The girls were silent for a moment as they took in the sounds of nature. Nancy could hear birds singing and creatures rustling in the underbrush. She hoped a squirrel wouldn't hop out and surprise Tristram again.

A bend in the trail brought them face-to-face with a post-and-rail fence about four feet high. Beyond it was a cornfield filled with green stalks waving in the wind.

"That *is* a big jump," George admitted. "But I promised I'd go first, and I will."

Elsa's eyes sparkled mischievously. "You asked for it. Just don't jump on the corn, or the farmer will get mad."

Nancy held her breath as George positioned Derby about thirty feet back from the jump. Then she guided him toward the center of the fence.

Seconds later, Derby sailed over it, his golden coat and yellow mane bright against the green corn. George steered Derby to the border of the field, then turned to face her friends. "Just like flying," she declared, grinning triumphantly. "Who's next?"

"I'll go," Elsa said. "Barchester won't rest till he follows Derby." Moments later, Barchester's jet-black form leaped over the fence with inches to spare. "Your turn, Nancy," she added, joining George.

Nancy gritted her teeth. She was an experienced rider, but the fence was huge. Still, she was confident that Tristram wouldn't let her down.

Squeezing her legs against the saddle, she urged Tristram into the jump. He shot toward it, his body like an arrow. Nancy hunched forward as the huge animal launched himself into flight. *This is so cool,* she thought as the cornfield streaked up at her.

Tristram's hooves met the ground, and Nancy's eyes widened. A huge hole appeared under his left foot. Tristram lurched to his knees, with Nancy clinging to his neck. She couldn't let herself fall—or else she'd be trampled!

2

Stumbling into Danger

Nancy catapulted out of the saddle. Her face banged against Tristram's mane, but she held on to keep from falling under his legs. Tristram whinnied in fear as he struggled to stand up. Nancy held her breath as the mighty bay horse wobbled upward and hoisted his foot out of the hole.

Nancy exhaled against Tristram's neck as the horse steadied himself. She shimmied back into the saddle and grabbed the loose reins. A second later, the panicky Tristram crashed into the cornfield ahead.

"It's okay, Tristram," Nancy said in a soothing voice. She stopped him, then turned to look at her friends.

"Are you okay, Nancy?" Elsa asked.

"I'm fine. I just hope Tristram wasn't hurt." Nancy

guided him out of the cornfield, then jumped off to examine him for injuries. As she ran her fingers over his legs, she said, "He's lucky he didn't break a bone falling in that hole. But he seems fine. I don't see a scratch on him."

"I didn't notice that hole when I jumped the fence," George said.

"Me neither," Elsa said.

"Let me check it out." Nancy handed Tristram's reins to George. She walked over and inspected the hole. It was about a foot deep and wide, and it looked freshly dug. It also looked like the hole had been covered by a grid of sticks, which was now smashed. On top of the sticks were bits of grass. Someone had dug this hole on purpose!

Nancy beckoned to her friends. "This is so weird. Someone made this hole and then disguised it as smooth ground." She pointed to the grid. "See? They sprinkled grass on these sticks for camouflage. No one could see the hole until it was too late."

Elsa paled. "But who would want to hurt a horse . . . or a rider?"

"Has anyone ridden on this trail recently?" George asked. She looked at Elsa. "You and I were lucky. Our horses must have just missed it."

"I don't think any Green Spring kids came here today," Elsa answered. "We were busy practicing stadium jumping in the morning. But a bunch of us rode these trails yesterday, so this hole couldn't have been here then. People from all over the area ride through here, but I guess we were the first ones to land in the hole."

"Lucky us," George said dryly.

"So the hole was probably dug last night or this morning," Nancy reasoned, scanning the ground around it. "Do you guys have a minute? I want to see something."

George grinned. "Of course we'll wait. This is becoming a case, isn't it?"

Elsa brightened. "I'd forgotten you're a detective, Nancy. If anyone can figure out who did this, you can. I just hope this doesn't mean more danger for the campers and the camp."

Even though Nancy was only eighteen, she was already an accomplished detective. Bess and George, also eighteen, had helped her out many times. Nancy wasn't sure whether this hole more than just some isolated prank, but she wanted to check out the area for clues.

Nancy met Elsa's worried gaze. "Has anything weird been happening around Green Spring?" she asked.

"Well . . . ," Elsa began. "I haven't known of any other traps like that hole, but some strange things *have* been happening at camp. For instance . . ." She paused for a moment, and began speaking in a whisper. "Promise you guys won't tell anyone outside the camp? I just don't want to hurt Green Spring's reputation by blabbing about what happened."

"Of course I won't tell," Nancy assured her.

"Me neither," George said.

"Well, just this morning, the girth to a girl's saddle snapped while she was stadium jumping," Elsa explained. "The saddle slid off with Juliana on it. She fell right under the horse! It was a miracle she wasn't hurt."

"Was the leather worn? Could it have broken on its own?" Nancy wondered.

Elsa sighed. "No way. It was a brand-new saddle, and the cut in the girth was straight. Only a razor or a knife could have done that. The person who did it must have left a small part of the leather attached so Juliana would put on the saddle without noticing the cut."

"Juliana must have freaked," George said.

"You bet. And that's not the only thing that's happened." Elsa blew out her breath, then continued. "Two days ago, we found poison ivy mixed in with some horses' feed."

"Did the horses eat it?" Nancy asked her.

"A few of them did," Elsa said, "and they were fine. Fortunately, horses aren't allergic to poison ivy. They eat it in fields all the time and never get sick. But the counselor who handled it broke out in a rash.

She was so upset, she quit this morning."

All these things sound serious, Nancy thought. *Whoever is doing them has to be stopped before people—or horses—get hurt.* "Is that it?" Nancy asked.

Elsa frowned. "Isn't that enough? I mean, just before lunch today, three campers left because they were so creeped out by all the stuff that's happened."

"I don't blame them," George said. "I'm sure the kids are wondering whose saddle girth is going to go next."

"Mrs. Rogers gave everyone strict orders to check horses, tack, stalls—everything—for safety before we ride," Elsa explained. "The most frustrating thing is that camp used to be so much fun. Now it's a downer. These accidents have affected everyone's mood."

"One thing's for sure," Nancy said firmly, "they're not accidents."

"Let's fill in this hole so no one else gets hurt, and then I've got to get back to the stable," Elsa said. "Dressage practice starts in half an hour, and I'm coaching."

Once they'd returned to Green Spring, the girls unsaddled their horses, rubbed them down, then let them loose in a field to graze. Nancy took her helmet off and shook out her shoulder-length reddish blond hair.

"Let's go find Mrs. Rogers," Elsa suggested,

putting the helmets in a tack room box. "I want to tell her about that trap."

The girls found Mrs. Rogers working in her office in a corner of the barn. A small, plump woman of about sixty-five, with apple red cheeks and gray hair wrapped in a bun, Mrs. Rogers threw a dazzling smile at the girls as they stepped in the door. "Welcome!" she said in a hearty voice, standing up to greet them. "How nice, Elsa, to bring friends."

After the introductions were made, Mrs. Rogers studied Nancy. "Are you by any chance Carson Drew's daughter?" she asked her.

"I am," Nancy said, smiling.

"I met your father at a party at Josh Bryant's house," Mrs. Rogers said brightly. "Josh's farm is across the valley from mine. The party was a fundraiser for his own riding program, and Josh invited all the people he thought might contribute to it. Since your dad is a busy lawyer, he was high on Josh's guest list. Your father's a charming man, Nancy. You look quite a lot like him. I've no doubt you're a chip off the old block."

"Thank you," Nancy said.

"Did you girls have a nice ride?" Mrs. Rogers asked.

Elsa told Mrs. Rogers about the booby trap.

"Why, Tristram could have broken his leg!" Mrs. Rogers said, horrified. "Are you sure he's okay?"

"He's fine," Nancy assured her. "He didn't limp at all on the way home."

"Mrs. Rogers," Elsa said, "whoever set that trap might also be the one who cut Juliana's girth and mixed the poison ivy into the feed. He, or she, is really getting dangerous."

Mrs. Rogers drew herself up, her blue eyes resolute. "*Getting* dangerous? This person was dangerous from day one! Juliana could have been killed when her saddle broke. We've got to find out who's doing these things—and fast." Her gaze turned to Nancy. "Correct me if I'm wrong, Nancy, but I'm now remembering your father telling me that you're an amateur detective. He seemed very proud of your sleuthing abilities."

Nancy laughed. "Well, you know how dads can be." She met Mrs. Rogers's gaze. She knew what the camp director was about to ask: whether she would help solve the mystery. Nancy was eager to say yes, but how could she investigate without all the campers realizing her role? If she was going to do a good job, she'd have to go undercover.

Mrs. Roger seemed to read Nancy's mind. "I hate to intrude on your busy life, Nancy, but is there a chance you could help me out? You could go undercover as a counselor here so no one would know you're investigating."

"Brilliant idea!" Elsa exclaimed. Her skin flushed

with excitement. "But what about George? She'd be a help, too. Could she be a counselor too?"

"What do you say, George?" Mrs. Rogers asked.

"Count me in—if Nancy agrees," George said.

Nancy gave George a quick thumbs-up sign before Mrs. Rogers continued. "A counselor quit this morning, so our little ruse will make sense. I'll say I'm hiring George as an extra counselor because we need all the help we can get to prepare for the upcoming rally. I assume you girls have adequate experience with horses?"

"Enough not to blow our cover," George said, pausing for a minute. "Well, as long as we don't teach dressage," she confessed.

Before Mrs. Rogers could comment, loud voices cut through their conversation. A boy and girl were arguing in the tack room next door about their riding skills.

Mrs. Rogers and the three girls froze as they listened to the heated conversation. "Face it, Rafael, your family's broke! You can't afford to match me. I'll always be a better rider than you—and you know it."

3

One Weird Warning

Mrs. Rogers's kind face suddenly hardened with anger. With her fists at her sides, she marched into the tack room. Nancy, George, and Elsa followed. A dark-haired boy of about sixteen stormed by them, his black eyes blazing. A girl about his age stood by the window, her mouth set in a triumphant smirk. As she saw Mrs. Rogers, she blanched, and her mouth twisted into an unattractive scowl.

Mrs. Rogers didn't bother to get the girl's side of the story. "Clare, I heard what you said to Rafael. Your attitude is inexcusable! It's worse than arrogant. It's unkind. What makes you think you're any better than he is?"

The girl shook back her long dark hair. "I'm sorry, Mrs. Rogers," she said. Her gold eyes defiantly met Mrs. Rogers's gaze.

She sure doesn't seem sorry, Nancy thought.

"Your rudeness to that boy and to the other scholarship campers has to stop," Mrs. Rogers told her. "One more mean remark and you're Green Spring history! I don't care how talented a rider you are."

Clare's voice was sullen. "I understand, Mrs. Rogers. I apologize."

"Apologize to Rafael, not to me," Mrs. Rogers snapped. "Now hurry to dressage. You're late for practice."

"Yes, Mrs. Rogers," Clare said calmly. She headed out.

Nancy, George, and Elsa followed Mrs. Rogers back to her office. Once there, Elsa telephoned Bess to tell her about the job at *The Horse's Mouth*. When Elsa hung up, she was smiling. "Just as I suspected, Bess is thrilled," Elsa told them. "I gave her the editor's name and number. She's going to call him right away." She headed over to the door. "Now, I'd better get over to dressage."

Elsa hurried out, and Mrs. Rogers began to explain the camp schedule to Nancy and George. When she'd finished, Nancy asked her about Clare.

"Clare Wu is a classic snob," Mrs. Rogers said in a tone of disgust. "She's arrogant, controlling, and drop-dead beautiful. I think she has a secret crush on Rafael, but he doesn't return it. She's not used to rejection, so I can see how it could make her mad."

"And that's why she's so mean to him?" George asked.

"The situation is complicated," Mrs. Rogers admitted. "Rafael Estevez is a very talented rider. My scholarship kids are every bit as qualified as the other campers. But he doesn't rate with Clare, because his family isn't wealthy. I don't publicize who the scholarship kids are—it's kept confidential—but somehow the kids all know who's who. It bothers Clare that she's attracted to someone she thinks isn't high class."

"I don't blame Rafael for not liking Clare when she's so horrible to him," Nancy said.

"Clare can be nice when it suits her," Mrs. Rogers said, "and she was nice to Rafael at first. But he's a quiet kid. He keeps to himself. Clare probably thought she was being tolerant and good-hearted by courting a boy from a different background, but when he didn't pay attention to her, she got mad. She thought Rafael should feel grateful she liked him. This is a lot of inference on my part, true, but most of it seems pretty obvious."

"Man, what a viper!" George exclaimed.

"I've been trying to manage her for the past three years at this camp, and she just gets worse each year. That girl is one big headache. But a lot of kids seem drawn to her. I wish I knew why."

"Charisma," Nancy said. "I bet it lets her get away with stuff."

"I just hope that 'stuff' doesn't include digging holes and cutting saddle girths," Mrs. Rogers said grimly.

"One thing's for sure," George said. "Clare's charisma won't blind Nancy. If Clare's guilty, Nancy'll find out."

In a short time, Nancy and George learned everything they needed to know about their counselor jobs from Mrs. Rogers. By now it was late afternoon; time to drive home to pack for camp.

As the two girls headed toward River Heights in Nancy's blue Mustang, the summer sun glittered in the western sky. They'd promised Mrs. Rogers to be back at Green Spring after dinner so they could meet the kids before bed. As she dropped George off, Nancy asked, "Can you have dinner at my house, George? At around six o'clock? Hannah said she'd make fried chicken. I'll see if Bess is free too."

"Awesome! I'm addicted to Hannah's chicken."

Hannah Gruen was the Drews' housekeeper. She had been part of the family since the death of Nancy's mother, when Nancy was three. Hannah's talent in the kitchen was not lost on Nancy and her two best friends.

"Should I pick you up in my car?" Nancy asked.

"Nah. I'll just walk over to your house after I pack," George said. "But could we pick up my duffel bag at my house on our way back to camp? That way, I won't have to haul it with me."

"Sure thing," Nancy said. George jumped out of the car and jogged down the path to her door.

George and Bess showed up on Nancy's doorstep promptly at six. "Come in!" Nancy said happily. "Hannah's chicken smells great. Dad had to work late, unfortunately."

"We'll leave some for him," George said.

"Excuse me? Hannah's chicken? Leftovers?" Bess said skeptically. "No way, José." Nancy smiled and went to get sodas for her friends.

"So did you interview for that job at *The Horse's Mouth?*" Nancy asked when she returned. "The one Elsa called you about?"

Bess's blue eyes danced. "Sure did. And I got the job!"

"Awesome," Nancy said, and grinned.

"Congratulations, Bess," George said. "That was fast. When do you start?"

"I already have. Mr. Blackstone, the editor, put me to work on the spot. He's pretty much snowed under, so he was happy I could spend an hour today helping him open mail."

"What are your other duties?" Nancy asked.

Bess grinned. It was clear that her new job thrilled

25

her. "I'm the editor of a column on equestrian fashion. It's called 'Looking Hot to Trot.' It has the cutest heading—an illustration of two horses, boy and girl, dressed up in Victorian clothing. Mr. Blackstone is going to write it, but if I get good at doing the research, he'll let me take over."

"Will you get your own byline?" Nancy asked.

"You bet," Bess said.

"My cousin the reporter," George said approvingly. "You'll be famous in River Heights."

Bess giggled. "In the horse world, at least—if I'm lucky."

"Did you have to dress up in a black hat and boots to prove you know about riding fashion?" George teased.

"My new pink miniskirt and purple tank top showed Mr. Blackstone that I'm a fashion expert." Bess glanced down at her outfit fondly.

"Hey, girls," Hannah called from the kitchen. "Soup's on."

Nancy, George, and Bess set the kitchen table while Hannah brought out fried chicken, freshly baked bread, and a green salad. Nancy quickly sat down with her friends. "Thanks, Hannah," she said, passing the chicken. "This looks great."

"It's my secret recipe," Hannah said proudly, returning to the kitchen.

"Speaking of secret," Bess said, leaning toward

Nancy and George, "I opened the strangest letter for Mr. Blackstone today. It was an anonymous note criticizing Green Spring Farm and Mrs. Rogers's camp."

"What did it say?" Nancy asked.

"First, that the riding lessons at Green Spring are bogus," Bess said, counting off on her fingers. "Second, that Mrs. Rogers doesn't know a horse from a cow, and third, that the stable isn't up to fire safety codes. But Elsa's taught at the camp for a couple summers, and she's totally loved it." Bess buttered a piece of bread and shrugged. "Mr. Blackstone thought the note was completely lame, but he's investigating the charges just in case."

Nancy and George exchanged glances. "That note is obviously just one more effort to trash Green Spring," Nancy said. She and George briefed Bess on Green Spring's problems and their decision to go undercover to investigate them.

The girls heard Hannah clear her throat from the kitchen. "Nancy, I want you and George to be careful," she warned. "This person sounds dangerous."

"I promise we'll be careful, Hannah," Nancy assured her. "But only if you'll give us some of your chocolate cake." She caught a glimpse of Hannah frosting a brown cake.

"That's a small price to pay," Hannah said, icing the last bit of cake with a flourish.

After finishing dessert the girls helped Hannah

clean up and thanked her for dinner. Then Nancy picked up her packed duffel bag from the luggage rack in her room, and she and her friends headed outside. Nancy and George waved good-bye to Bess as she drove away, then they headed for Nancy's Mustang in her driveway.

Suddenly, Nancy stopped and pulled on George's arm. "Look!" she said, pointing at her car. White swirls of soapy writing covered the back windshield. "Get away from Green Spring, Nancy Drew!" it warned. At the end of the message, a picture of a horse's head crossed with a gigantic X glared at the girls.

4

Fire!

"How could anyone know I'm investigating?" Nancy asked.

"Someone must have overheard our conversation with Mrs. Rogers and followed us here," George said.

"Clare was in the tack room next door when Mrs. Rogers hired us," Nancy said. "Clare looks around sixteen; I bet she has her driver's license. She could have driven here, soaped the windows, and then driven back to camp."

"We'll have to ask some campers if they saw her," George said. "She would have been gone at least an hour."

Nancy sighed, feeling frustrated. "So our cover's blown already. Still, we might as well stay on as counselors. Even if the person knows what we're up to, we'll be in a better position to catch him or her if we're working at Green Spring."

"We might make him nervous just by being there," George said hopefully. "Maybe he won't try anything dangerous again."

Nancy thought George was being overly optimistic. Whoever was playing these tricks didn't seem the least bit nervous. Quite the opposite, in fact. The person seemed highly dangerous, and the only way to change that would be to catch him or her.

After cleaning off the windshield Nancy and George slid into the front seat of the car. They picked up George's duffel bag at her house before driving out to Green Spring Farm. It was nestled in a beautiful valley, among rolling hills and woods.

Once there, Nancy and George took a moment to scan the grounds. The only building at Green Spring aside from the bighouse was the stable. It was huge, with an indoor riding ring in the center surrounded by stalls, the tack room, a feed room, and Mrs. Rogers's office. A wide corridor with a soft earth floor separated the stalls from the ring. Outside the barn were several green pastures, where horses grazed during the day; two outdoor riding rings with white wooden fences; and a dressage ring. Now the pastures were empty, but Nancy and George could see horses gazing over their stall doors.

"We'd better get up to the house," Nancy said. "It must be almost time for lights-out."

The girls carried their duffels up the gravel path to the gigantic stone house with its four turrets, bay windows, wraparound porch, and overgrown gardens. "What a great place," George commented. "It looks like at one point it was really in pristine condition, but now its owner cares more about horses than being featured in some glossy home decorating magazine."

As Mrs. Rogers opened the door, a pack of dogs and cats rushed out of the house to greet them. "Scruffy, down!" she commanded. "You too, Inky and Nutmeg. And Marmalade, I'm watching you. You're *way* too friendly for a cat."

Sure enough, an orange cat with white stripes leaped up at the girls along with the dogs. "Marmalade thinks he's canine," Mrs. Rogers told them. She unwrapped a skinny brown creature from her shoulder and added, "Unlike Kula here, who knows he's a ferret. Anyway, come on in and meet the others!"

"Human, or animal?" George joked, as she patted the wiggly ferret.

"Both," Mrs. Rogers said. She led them into the wide front hall. At the bottom of the mahogany stairway, the banister post was carved to look like a fox. Gothic archways in the hall opened onto parlors and a dining room, where campers were busy snacking, playing board games, watching videos on two TVs, and playing hide-and-go-seek. The furniture, a mix of antiques and tag sale finds, lay scattered in a comfortable jumble around the rooms. It was clear to Nancy that kids and animals ruled in this house!

"Bedtime, kids," Mrs. Rogers proclaimed. A collective groan rose from the campers. "Don't forget—I'm announcing the rally team tomorrow. I'm not going to accept anyone who isn't well rested." With that, the campers began to stop their activities. Within a few minutes, they had assembled at the base of the stairs.

Mrs. Rogers raised her hand for attention. "Before you go up, I have some introductions to make. This is Nancy Drew and George Fayne. As you all know, we lost a counselor this morning, and these ladies are taking her place. I want you kids to behave for them." A sea of curious teenage faces gazed at Nancy and George. Mrs. Rogers finished by asking, "Have any of you seen Tarzan?"

A thin girl with platinum-blond hair said, "He and Inky got into a scuffle, so I put Tarzan in your room. Hope you don't mind."

"Not in the least," Mrs. Rogers said. Turning to Nancy and George, she explained, "Tarzan is my pet monkey, and Inky is my black Lab. They don't get along at all." She shot Inky, curled on a hallway chair, a withering look before leading everyone upstairs. She then retired to her room.

Elsa popped out of a bedroom door to greet Nancy and George. "I thought I heard your voices. I'm so glad you're here! Let me introduce you to the other counselor, James Fenwick—behind you."

Nancy and George turned to see a cute guy with chestnut hair and gray eyes standing in the upstairs hall. "Elsa told me you were coming," he said. "Let me know if you need any help or anything. But please excuse me now; I'm supervising the boys' room, and they seem especially wired tonight." He slipped through a nearby door.

"Everybody's off-the-wall tonight," Elsa said, craning to check out a pillow fight in her room. "They're excited about the team announcement tomorrow. Anyway, Mrs. Rogers asked me to show you to your rooms. You'll be sharing them with some campers."

Once they were farther down the hall, Elsa explained, "Mrs. Rogers has her own bedroom and bathroom on this floor." She pointed to a closed door at the front of the house. "Besides hers, there are four rooms on this floor and four upstairs. And of course, there are bathrooms on every floor." She stopped all of a sudden. "Here are your rooms."

Elsa gestured to two doors across the hall from each other. "George, you're on the left, Nancy, on the right. I'll see you guys in the morning."

Nancy said good night to George and Elsa and went into her room. Three girls, each about sixteen years old, stared at her from their canopied beds. "Hi," Nancy said. "I'm Nancy Drew. I've been assigned to your room."

"We know," said a stocky girl with curly blond hair. "I'm Cordelia Zukerman, by the way."

"Your bed's over there," a tall girl with long braids said, pointing to the corner. "Make yourself comfortable. Oh, and I'm Akiyah Hopkins."

"Nice to meet both of you," Nancy said. Turning to the third girl, who was dark-haired with high cheekbones and a shy smile, Nancy said, "What is your name?"

"Juliana Suarez," she answered softly. The girl with the broken girth, Nancy remembered.

"How many campers are there in all?" Nancy asked, tossing her duffel bag on her bed.

"There are supposed to be twenty-four campers, three counselors, and Mrs. Rogers," Akiyah explained. "But today we lost three kids and a counselor and added one kid and you two counselors. I've lost count!"

"How does Mrs. Rogers take care of so many kids?" Nancy asked.

"The three C's: cooks, cleaners, and counselors," Cordelia said flatly. "They keep the camp running so Mrs. Rogers doesn't have a heart attack from too much work. Still, this place can get pretty wild, especially in the evenings, when we kids and all the animals are thrown together. Did you see Flower, Mrs. Rogers's raccoon? Every night she escapes from her cage to sleep in the living room fireplace. That's pretty weird, if you ask me."

Nancy arched a brow. "Things do seem kind of eccentric around here—in a fun way," she added.

"Camp is tons of fun," Juliana said. Her face clouded over. "At least, until yesterday . . ."

"I heard about your saddle," Nancy said. "I'm glad you're okay. By the way, do you guys know Clare Wu well?"

Nancy's roommates exchanged glances. "You mean Clare 'Snotty' Wu who thinks she's so pretty and cool?" Cordelia said. "Why are you curious about her?"

"She was yelling at this boy earlier," Nancy explained. "I think his name is Rafael. I just wondered if she was always so chilly."

Akiyah snorted. "She was always a tough girl. None of us like her at all."

"She has this clique of friends," Cordelia said. "Some of them are George's roommates. Clare is sharing a room upstairs with a couple more 'Clare worshipers.' I don't know why anyone likes her—but they do. Of course, none of her friends talk to us, so I can't find out why they think she rules." She threw up her hands. "It's a mystery."

Nancy pulled a nightgown and toothbrush from her duffel bag and tossed them on her bed. "Not really. Some people probably like her because she's rich and pretty. They think she has power, and that some of it will rub off on them." Nancy was tempted to ask whether any of the girls had seen Clare snooping around Juliana's saddle or messing with the horses' feed, but she didn't want to plant the idea that Clare might be guilty. Instead, she asked, "Did you guys notice whether Clare was here around dinnertime?"

"Clare's been away since the late afternoon," Akiyah said. "I don't think she's even back yet. She got special permission to spend the evening in town with her brother. He's leaving for college tomorrow."

"Does she drive?" Nancy asked.

"Yup—her own little convertible Porsche her daddy gave her," Cordelia said in a mocking tone.

Nancy bit her lip. So Clare could have followed her back home and soaped her windshield. But what did Clare have against Green Spring?

"Hey, what's that smell?" Juliana asked, sitting up in bed.

Nancy sniffed. "Smoke!" she cried. She rushed to the open window where the breeze was blowing in

36

the hideous smell. As she looked outside and down the hill, she saw orange and yellow flames billowing from a corner of the barn. "The barn's on fire. The horses!" Nancy shouted, springing out the door.

5

Tack Attack

Nancy ran out of the room and pounded on Mrs. Rogers's door. "Mrs. Rogers, wake up! The barn's on fire!"

The door flung open, and a bleary-eyed Mrs. Rogers came running out, still shuffling on her loafers. "I just called the fire department. We've got to save the horses!"

Kids were streaming out of their rooms and throwing on robes and shoes. "Campers!" Mrs. Rogers barked. "You stay here, for your own safety. Counselors, come with me."

James hurried out of his room wearing jeans and an inside-out T-shirt. Elsa, George, and Nancy joined him on the stairs, still in their regular clothes.

In less than two minutes they were evacuating the horses from the barn.

"Just open the stall doors that lead into the field," Mrs. Rogers commanded, throwing open Derby's door. The flames sizzled and crackled nearby. "If the horses refuse to come out, blindfold them with these and force them to follow you." She handed a bunch of rags to each counselor.

Nancy was relieved to see that the fire was confined to the corner feed room, but with the breeze blowing and hay and straw everywhere, the flames would surely spread fast.

Tristram bolted by Nancy into the field as the welcome sound of sirens blared through the night. Seconds later, two fire trucks were hosing down the barn.

Smoke filled the air as the firefighters worked. When the last ember had finally fizzled out, the fire chief turned off his hose and strode over to Mrs. Rogers. "Lucky you called us so quick, Mrs. R.," he said. "We got here just in time. Most of the damage is confined to that corner." He pointed to the feed room.

Mrs. Rogers sighed. "I can't thank you enough. It's your prompt work that saved the barn." She shuddered. "Thank goodness it's the feed room that burned, and not a horse's stall." She led everyone over to the charred room to inspect it. The sharp

40

smell of burnt grain filled Nancy's nose.

"Obviously the feed is destroyed," Mrs. Rogers said, looking around. "We'll need to get more before the horses' breakfast tomorrow. But I was lucky. Nothing aside from the wall next to the feed was destroyed."

The fire chief walked over to a pile of ashes and flakes of burlap. "Looks like the fire started here," he said.

"We piled empty feed sacks in that corner," Mrs. Rogers explained. "Also, Green Spring's flag was there." A shred of green and gold fabric on a bent metal pole poked out of the ashes. "Can you tell how it started?"

The fire chief knelt down and studied the area. Then he asked Mrs. Rogers whether lamps and other electrical devices had been in the room.

"Just an overhead lightbulb," she declared.

"Unfortunately, I can't tell how the fire started," the chief said. "If someone set it with a match, there'd be no evidence left."

Mrs. Rogers blanched. "'Set it?' You mean on purpose?"

As they spoke, Nancy scanned the room for clues. If someone had set the fire on purpose, it was possible a clue had been dropped. If it was metal, it could have survived the fire. But she only saw charred wood, ashes, and bent metal feed cans. Nancy moved by the

41

sooty windowsill to study the contents of the cans, but a flicker behind the broken window made her stop. Someone's shadow?

Before she could blink, it was gone. Nancy ran outside. The full moon lit up the field in which a group of frightened horses huddled. Beyond the field, dark woods rose against the sky. Whoever had slipped by the window had disappeared into the night.

Maybe it was one of the firefighters checking for sparks, Nancy thought. She hurried to the other side of the barn, where a group of firefighters was busy making sure no embers had spread. "Were any of you guys just around on the other side?" Nancy asked them.

One man glanced around at the crew and said, "Nope. We're all accounted for here, except the chief—he's with Mrs. Rogers."

Just then, Nancy remembered the note that Bess had opened at *The Horse's Mouth*. It had charged Green Spring's barn with not being up to fire safety standards. "Does this barn get inspected every year for fire safety?" Nancy asked the same man.

"Sure does," he answered. "In fact, we inspected this barn about four months ago. It was up to code, no doubt about it. Mrs. Rogers keeps this place ship-shape. The fire damage tonight might have been a lot worse otherwise."

Nancy thanked the man for the information, then walked back to the feed room. She ran into George on the way.

"The fire chief's wrapping things up with Mrs. Rogers," George told Nancy. "She told the counselors to go back to the house. The horses will stay in the field for the night, just to be on the safe side. At least it's nice out."

Nancy and George strolled back to the house side by side, with Elsa and Jimmy straggling behind. "That fire was pretty suspicious," Nancy said. "I saw a shadow at the feed room window. I think someone was spying—maybe to find out how bad the damage was."

George shook her head. "Those horses could have been killed. I mean, who would set a fire like that on purpose?"

"We know this person doesn't care about horses or people. Whoever's doing all this is out to wreck Green Spring no matter what's in the way." Nancy then recalled a possible clue. "Clare Wu was away from camp tonight, supposedly seeing her brother. She could have soaped my windshield—and also set the fire."

"You think she would have put her own horse in danger?" George wondered. "That's as low as you can go."

"We'll have to find out where her horse's stall is.

Maybe she was planning to free him if the fire got too close." Nancy opened the front door of the house to the sight of petrified campers grouped in the hall.

"Are the horses okay?" Akiyah asked in a whisper.

Nancy reassured the kids about the horses and the barn. Despite her soothing words, she could tell the campers' nerves were rattled. As Nancy tried to calm one girl, she abruptly turned away. "I don't care what anyone says—I'm *so* out of here. Mom and Dad can just come and get me tonight." She stalked to a telephone at the back of the hall.

As the other campers trudged back up the stairs, a pair of gold almond-shaped eyes caught Nancy's attention. Clare was back from her brother's.

Light streamed in through the window and woke Nancy at seven. Juliana and Akiyah were already putting on blue jeans and ankle-length riding boots. Juliana zipped a pair of brown suede chaps over her worn jeans.

"Nancy, will you please wake Cordelia?" Akiyah asked. "She'll get mad at us if we do it. You're an authority figure, so she won't mess with you."

Nancy smiled and straggled out of bed to wake Cordelia. Then she put on blue jeans, boots, and a sky-blue T-shirt that matched her eyes. A delicious smell wafted into their room. "Pancakes," Cordelia announced, hurrying into the hall in unlaced boots.

"We'd better get down there quick."

Sure enough, a pile of steaming blueberry pancakes awaited everyone. Sounds of giggling and jokes rose through the dining room as campers and counselors ate. After taking a bite of a pancake and swallowing it down, Nancy leaned over to George. "The mood here seems much better today," she whispered.

"The rally team is being announced at lunch," George said. "Everyone's really excited about that."

Still using a low voice, Nancy said, "I want to search Clare's car after breakfast. I'm curious to see if there's evidence of soap or matches."

Once she was finished, Nancy cleared her plate and headed to the kitchen to find Mrs. Rogers. She wanted to ask her permission to search Clare's car. As Nancy passed through the pantry she was startled by a high-pitched chattering noise coming from the far corner.

"Nancy, meet Tarzan," Mrs. Rogers said, bustling out of the kitchen. "Most people think he's kind of obnoxious, but who knows? Maybe you two will be friends."

A gray monkey was attached to a playpen post by a collar and leash. He shook his fist at Nancy and screamed. "Somehow I don't think we click," Nancy said wryly.

Mrs. Rogers picked him up, and he wrapped his arms affectionately around her. "Don't worry, Nancy, you're not alone. For some reason, he tolerates me."

With Mrs. Rogers's permission—and she got it very easily—Nancy searched Clare's car. Unfortunately, she found no clues. She reported back to the director in her office. "If Clare *is* guilty, what could be her motive for harming your camp?" Nancy asked.

Mrs. Rogers puckered her brow. "Maybe she resents the scholarship program because my quota kept her from making last year's rally team. I have a rule that at least two spots go to scholarship campers."

After their conversation Nancy joined up with George, who was helping a boy measure grain in a temporary feed room set up in an empty stall. Once the boy left to feed his horse, George started speaking. "Elsa told me the camp schedule today. After the kids feed their horses and clean out stalls, they divide into two groups, Green and Gold—Green Spring's colors. This morning, I'm helping Elsa coach stadium jumping to the Green Group in the outdoor ring, while you, James, and Mrs. Rogers supervise the Gold Group cleaning tack and grooming horses. We switch activities in the afternoon."

"Thanks for the drill, Sergeant Fayne," Nancy joked.

George laughed, and the two friends parted ways. Nancy headed for the tack room and began to set out cans of saddle soap, sponges, and buckets of water for the Gold Group. After a few minutes, Rafael Estevez appeared in the doorway. "Hi, Nancy," he said. "I just finished feeding Clown and cleaning out his stall. The schedule says the Gold Group does tack now."

"The schedule never lies," Nancy declared. "Come on in, Rafael. I got the supplies ready."

But Rafael didn't reply. He was gaping at something behind her. Nancy whirled around. She saw only racks of saddles attached to the wall—nothing the least bit strange.

Rafael pushed past her and grabbed a saddle off a rack labeled CLOWN. His hands shook as he lowered it, and in a flash Nancy saw exactly what was wrong: The saddle had been ruined—gouged by a sharp object. Ugly scratches covered the once smooth caramel color of the leather seat.

Rafael threw his saddle on the floor and collapsed on a nearby stool. He buried his face in his hands. Nancy wanted to try to comfort him, but she knew she had to tell Mrs. Rogers what happened immediately. "I'll be right back, Rafael," she said, patting his shoulder. Then she hurried into the office next door.

"This is outrageous!" Mrs. Rogers said after Nancy had delivered the bad news. "Rafael worked an extra summer job to buy that saddle." Like a tiny gray tornado, Mrs. Rogers whirled into the tack room with

Nancy following. As Mrs. Rogers studied the saddle and questioned Rafael, Nancy searched the room for clues. A glint on the floor under the saddle rack caught her eye.

Nancy picked up the object. It was long, sharp, and thin, and it gleamed wickedly in the morning sun that poured through the window. But it wasn't a knife. It was a sterling silver letter opener, with the initials JB monogrammed on the handle.

6

A Mixed-up Message

"Look what I found," Nancy said.

Mrs. Rogers and Rafael looked carefully at the letter opener in Nancy's palm. Gingerly, the camp director took it, and Rafael rose from his stool to get a better look.

"Can you think of anyone who has the initials JB?" Nancy asked.

Mrs. Rogers pursed her lips. After a moment, she said, "There are three people at camp who have the first initial J—James Fenwick, Juliana Suarez, and Jessie Greenstein. And there's one camper with a last initial of B—Todd Brown. But no one with that combination." She studied the letter opener, holding it up to the light. Her eyes widened. "JB," she murmured, "I wonder if this could belong to Josh Bryant."

"Josh Bryant?" Nancy asked. "Isn't he the neighbor you mentioned yesterday? The one who had the party where you met my dad?"

"Sure is," Mrs. Rogers said. "Although 'neighbor' may be the wrong word. His farm is next to mine, but it takes a good half hour to ride there on horseback. The Kinderhook Creek separates our properties."

"Has he been over here recently?" Nancy asked.

"He came to the barn yesterday morning." She sighed. "It's a complicated story. See, Josh runs his own pony club and summer camp. But it's not a well-run program, and frankly, the campers don't seem very happy there. Josh is often losing kids to my program. My camp seems more popular." She smiled at Rafael. "You can be the judge of my words, Rafael. Am I bragging, or being unfair?"

"No way, Mrs. Rogers!" Rafael retorted. "Even if Mr. Bryant had a scholarship program and I could go there, I wouldn't. That place is a joke."

Some kids showed up at the tack room door. "The Gold Group has tack cleaning, right?" a girl asked.

"Yes," Mrs. Rogers said, sweeping Rafael's saddle behind her back before anyone could see the damage. "Why don't you kids get started here while I finish my conversation with Nancy and Rafael in my office. Nancy has set everything up for you." The campers left to get started.

In Mrs. Rogers's office, Nancy asked, "So why was Mr. Bryant at Green Spring yesterday?"

"To take back a horse he'd lent me," Mrs. Rogers replied. "He had a fit because Katie O'Donovan ditched his camp for mine, so he came to retrieve Goldbug to get back at me. Those were his very words. I would have been short a horse if Katie hadn't brought her own."

"Katie O'Donovan?" Nancy said. The name sounded familiar.

"She's a new camper. Arrived yesterday," Mrs. Rogers explained. "You might have met her up at the house. I believe she's in Elsa's room." Nancy had heard a lot of names mentioned during breakfast conversation, but she couldn't put a face to all of them yet.

"Why did Katie leave the other camp?" Nancy asked.

Mrs. Rogers shook her head. "It's a shame, really. Katie was Josh's favorite camper. She's a terrific rider, and she owns a star horse called Black Comet. But she left because his riding instruction disappointed her. Josh just couldn't get his act together to provide a challenge for a rider like her. I never recruited Katie, but Josh is the grudge-bearing type. He blames me for her leaving." She smiled slightly.

51

"Anyway, I doubt I'll be invited to another party of his anytime soon."

Nancy glanced from Mrs. Rogers's face to the letter opener in her palm. "So Mr. Bryant was here to take back his horse. But why would he have brought his letter opener with him?"

Mrs. Rogers shrugged. "Beats me. Unless he brought it here to vandalize a saddle in revenge for losing Katie." Her eyes darted toward the saddle rack. "I have a thought, Nancy. Black Comet's saddle is next to Clown's. Could Josh have meant to harm Katie's saddle, but got Rafael's by mistake?"

Nancy shot a look at the saddle racks, each one specifically labeled with the horse's name. "It would be hard to mix them up," Nancy said. "Maybe he meant to hurt Katie's saddle, but then heard someone coming and settled for Rafael's. It's a little closer to the door."

Mrs. Rogers nodded. "That makes sense." She turned to Rafael. "I feel responsible for your saddle, so please don't worry about replacing it—I'll handle that. Maybe Nancy could drive you to Equestrian Outfitters, the riding shop in River Heights, either today or tomorrow." She checked the wall clock. "Meanwhile, it's time to switch activities with the Green Group. Stadium jumping is next."

Ten minutes later, Nancy and Mrs. Rogers had joined James at one of the outdoor rings. Several

Gold Group riders had already congregated at the gate on their horses. Nancy studied the jumps in the ring. They included multicolored poles and barrels, imitation hedges and chicken coops, and a large white board painted with a blue and red bull's-eye. The first horse to make the round was Clown, with Rafael riding on a borrowed saddle.

Nancy and James cheered him on, but when Clown approached the bull's-eye, he skidded to the side and refused to jump it. James ducked through the ring fence to give Rafael some pointers. On the next try, Clown sailed over the bull's-eye beautifully.

One by one, the rest of the Gold Group campers took the jumps. Many of the horses were fine on the course, but some were skittish like Clown. "Horses really have their own personalities, just like us," James told Nancy. "Some freak out at these jumps. Others just want to get back to the barn and eat hay. Like Victoria here."

Nancy watched Victoria, Clare Wu's red roan mare, execute a perfect round. The moment Clare finished, Mrs. Rogers clapped Nancy and James on the back. "Time for lunch," she declared. "It's served at the house. I'm announcing the rally team, so the atmosphere's going to be tense."

"Was it a hard decision—picking the team?" Nancy asked.

"It was especially difficult this year," Mrs. Rogers

admitted. "We had some very good riders with miserable horses, and some not-so-great riders with wonderful horses. I did my best to choose a strong team. I only hope the kids who didn't make the team won't be too upset."

A half hour later, all the campers and counselors were eating lunch served buffet-style under a tent next to Mrs. Rogers's house. As Nancy and George sat down at a table with their plates full of pasta salad and hot dogs, Nancy felt the tension mounting over who made the team. A timid girl with wavy brown hair and glasses sat next to Nancy. She pushed the food around on her plate without eating it.

Nancy and George introduced themselves. "I'm Katie O'Donovan," the girl said without making eye contact. She stopped speaking as Mrs. Rogers walked up to the front of the tent and raised a hand to signal quiet.

The teens leaned toward her, their faces full of eagerness and dread. Mrs. Rogers began. "I'd like to congratulate all you campers on the fabulous improvement in your riding skills. From the beginning of camp until now, your progress has been amazing. You should all be proud, proud, proud! The rally team was very hard to choose this year because we had so many strong contenders. Anyway, I won't keep you in suspense any longer." She took a dramatic pause. "I'll start by announcing the team captain: Akiyah Hopkins!"

A burst of applause and cheers rang through the tent as Akiyah joined Mrs. Rogers. Mrs. Rogers gave her a warm hug. "Akiyah is a superb rider," she went on, "and I'm sure she'll make a great team captain. I'm stepping aside now so she can announce her teammates." Mrs. Rogers handed Akiyah an envelope and told her to read from the paper inside.

"Just like the Oscars," George murmured to Nancy.

With trembling fingers, Akiyah ripped open the envelope. Everyone hushed. She drew out the paper and scanned it. Her face tensed.

"No way can I announce this," she breathed. She dropped the note as if it were poison. It flew up in the gentle breeze, then landed facedown on the grass outside the tent.

7

Swept Away

Mrs. Rogers bent down and snatched up the note. Then she fished for her spectacles in her skirt pocket and jammed them onto her face. She squinted at the paper in her hand.

Suddenly her eyes hardened. She crumpled the paper angrily and thrust it into her pocket. "Girls and boys," she began, holding up her hand for silence. But the campers had erupted in a flurry of questions and speculations, and it took a moment to gather their attention.

"I wonder what that note said," George whispered to Nancy.

"You and me both," Nancy said. "We'll ask Mrs. Rogers when we're alone with her and can talk about the case."

"Excuse me!'" Mrs. Rogers shouted. She took a whistle out of her pocket and blew it. Everyone instantly hushed. "That's more like it! Anyway, I'm sorry to tell you kids that someone substituted a very inappropriate message for the names of the team. I'd like to postpone the announcement of the team until dinner tonight, when we're in a better mood to celebrate. We'll break up now into our regular afternoon activities. I believe the Gold Group has dressage, while the Green Group swims. Later there's cross-country for both groups."

A groan of disappointment filled the tent. Nancy watched Mrs. Rogers trudge into the house carrying an empty salad bowl and a platter of cookie crumbs. The campers began clearing their plates in silence. Everyone seemed too stunned to speak. Nancy and George followed Mrs. Rogers inside with empty pitchers and plates of leftover watermelon slices.

Nancy and George set the dishes on the kitchen counter where Mrs. Rogers had cleared a space. "Thank you so much for your help, girls," she said. She glanced sideways at the cook, who was putting food away. "Let's go into the dining room," she murmured. "I want some privacy while we discuss the note."

The girls sat down beside Mrs. Rogers at the dining room table. "Let me know what you make of this, Nancy," she said, pulling the crumpled paper from her pocket.

Nancy scanned the message, with George looking on. "Close down your camp—or tragedy will strike!" it read.

Nancy handed the paper back to Mrs. Rogers. "This message is threatening more danger. I think we should call the police. But I'll continue with my investigation."

"I'll call them right away," Mrs. Rogers said. Just then, two girls who were fourteen years old entered the room. One girl looked defiant, and the other was rubbing tears from her eyes.

"Mrs. Rogers, Rebecca and I want to go home," the first girl said. "It's getting too creepy around here. Camp ends tomorrow, anyway."

"I'm really scared here," Rebecca whimpered.

Mrs. Rogers looked crushed, but she forced a smile. "I'm sorry you girls want to leave. But by all means, call your parents to bring you home if you feel in danger. I think you're safe here, though. And I'm about to call the police, to ensure our safety."

Rebecca shuddered. "The police? Things must be even worse than I'd thought. I'd like to call Mom and Dad right now, if you don't mind."

As Mrs. Rogers led them into the kitchen, Nancy and George exchanged glances. "If I don't solve this case soon, Mrs. Rogers won't have a camp," Nancy said gravely.

"We need more clues," George said, "and more suspects. Clare's our only one."

"She and JB," Nancy said. She briefed George on Rafael's saddle, and finding the letter opener with the JB monogram. Just as she finished her story, Mrs. Rogers returned to the room.

"Chief McGinnis is on his way here with an associate, Officer Rivken," Mrs. Rogers explained. "Unfortunately, Rebecca and Natalie have gone upstairs to pack." She threw up her hands in a weary gesture. "I guess the only thing for us to do now is get on with our afternoon activities."

Chief McGinnis soon showed up with Officer Rivken, a slim, dark-haired young man with alert brown eyes. Nancy, who was helping the Gold Group prepare for dressage, waved to the officers as they approached the ring. "I can give you all the information I have so far," she offered.

"Don't blow your cover by talking to us for too long," Chief McGinnis warned. "Mrs. Rogers has already given us the lowdown."

"My cover's blown already," Nancy said. She told the officers about the soaped message on her windshield. "But you're right, Chief McGinnis. It's better if most of the kids don't realize I'm a detective."

Officer Rivken nodded in agreement. "If they feel like you're a regular person, you'll catch more gossip from them. And the more information you can get, the better."

Nancy told them her suspicions about Clare, and also about finding the letter opener. Then the policemen set off to search the house and barn for clues.

The Gold Group finished its dressage session with Rafael taking Clown through his paces. Nancy watched the horse execute tight circles and loops in various gaits, from a walk, to a trot, to a slow canter. Letters posted around the ring marked places where the horse should change its gait.

Rafael shifted in his saddle, giving his horse subtle commands. Every movement of horse and rider was pitch perfect. "It's like a dance, like an old-fashioned minuet done by a horse," Nancy whispered to James, who was coaching.

"I prefer stadium jumping and cross-country," James said. "They're more exciting. But dressage is just as important to the overall rally score."

Suddenly they heard a voice behind them. Nancy recognized Clare's nasal tone. Turning, she saw Clare talking to a blond girl as they sat on their horses waiting for dressage to finish. "Will Rafael ever get Clown to go from a walk directly into a canter? He always lets him trot in between," Clare complained.

"Give him a break, Clare," the blond girl said. "Clown is Mrs. Rogers's horse, anyway. Rafael isn't used to him the way you're used to Victoria."

Clare rolled her eyes. "I don't care, Emmy. He thinks he's this great rider and he's not. I'm glad his saddle got trashed. Serves him right for being such a jerk."

"Wow, Clare, stop right there. That's harsh," the blond girl said. "Anyway, Rafael's finishing up, and he was the last of our group to go. It's our turn to swim." The girls took off for the barn at a brisk trot. Nancy and James exchanged glances.

"That Clare is something, huh?" he said.

"At least her friend told her off," Nancy remarked.

"Are you kidding?" James said wryly. "Emily's comment meant nothing to Clare. Clare never clues in when she's being dissed. I guess she thinks she's too cool for criticism. It goes right over her head. Though I don't now how, because it's so big."

Nancy laughed. "Anyway, it's a hot day. I'm looking forward to that swim." With that, she followed Rafael out of the ring.

Swimming and cross-country practice went smoothly that afternoon. At the end of the day Nancy returned to the house to shower. Dinner was informal, but Nancy put on a short, peach-colored skirt, white tank top, and sandals. It was just so hot. She swept her reddish-blond hair off her neck and secured it with a black elastic band.

Downstairs, she found George in white jeans and a black tank top serving herself tomato salad and a cheeseburger. "Get in line quick, Nan, before the hordes arrive," George advised.

Nancy slipped behind George just before a group of campers streamed into the tent. The two girls took seats at one of the picnic tables and began to eat. Nancy could tell that everyone was eagerly waiting for Mrs. Rogers to attempt once again to announce the team.

The camp director arrived in the midst of a dog pack. They all made their way to the front of the tent. "They want dinner, too," she explained as the dogs panted and wiggled around her. "But I don't want to keep you kids in suspense any longer. This time, we don't have a list to read. I've *told* Akiyah who her teammates are. She'll make the announcement now."

As Mrs. Rogers sat down from the small podium, Akiyah stepped up. "I'm proud to announce the Green Spring Pony Club's thirtieth annual rally team. Besides myself, we have"—she cleared her throat, then finished—"Katie O'Donovan, Rafael Estevez, and Clare Wu—with Cordelia Zukerman as stable manager."

Cheers and claps erupted through the tent as the rest of the team moved up to the front and joined Akiyah. There were only a few muffled moans of disappointment. As the team thanked Mrs. Rogers, Nancy leaned toward George. "I'm pretty full—and right now I'd really like to search Clare's room while I've got the chance."

"I'll save you a Popsicle," George promised. "Grape or orange?"

"Orange," Nancy said, smiling. "Thanks, George. And I'll let you know what I find." After clearing her plate, Nancy went upstairs. She remembered that Clare's room was on the third floor.

Nancy reached the third-floor hall without being seen by anyone. She peered into the room nearest the stairs. Her heart beat faster. Taped onto one of the dresser mirrors were several snapshots of Clare riding Victoria. *This is it!* Nancy thought, excited.

A sudden gust of wind whipped through an open window and swirled the pages of a comic book lying on a nearby table. Nancy glanced outside. Black clouds covered the sky, and a streak of lightning zipped to the ground. The world lit up like an X ray, then instantly darkened. Nancy had to turn on a light to search Clare's dresser—and she knew she had to work fast. Once it started raining, the campers would come inside.

The top two drawers of the dresser held clothes, but the third drawer was a jumble of papers, letters, more snapshots, and a notebook with Clare's name on the front. Nancy picked it up. On the first page, the words MY DIARY were written in capital letters.

But the rest of the page was in code! Not exactly pig latin, Nancy decided, but close.

Lightning streaked through the sky again, and the lights flickered. Gasps came from downstairs as the electricity died. Nancy bit her lip in frustration. Now it was too dark to read, much less decipher Clare's code. She put the notebook back and shut the drawer. Why would Clare bother to write in code if she wasn't guilty of *something*?

A refreshing breeze woke Nancy the next morning. Storms from the night before had wiped out all the heat. At breakfast, Mrs. Rogers announced that the team would separate from the rest of the campers for intensive practice. They'd leave for the rally tomorrow.

As she helped clear the breakfast dishes, Nancy told Mrs. Rogers about Clare's diary. "I'm getting nowhere with Clare, Mrs. Rogers," she added. "I'd like to widen my investigation. Maybe George and I could ride over to Josh Bryant's house and hunt around for clues. I'll bring the letter opener and ask him if it's his."

"Oh Nancy, be careful!" Mrs. Rogers cried. "Josh Bryant can be a spirited, mean man if ever there was one. Also, if you go on horseback, you'll have to cross the Kinderhook Creek that separates our farms. After last night's storm, the water will be turbulent." She pursed her lips. "Come into the kitchen with me—I'll draw you a map. I know a shallow spot where you should be able to cross the creek safely."

An hour later, Nancy and George were on their way to Josh Bryant's farm on Tristram and Derby. George had offered to carry a small backpack filled with bottled water, halters, lead ropes, and the silver letter opener. The girls rode through fields and down forest trails, always following Mrs. Rogers's map that Nancy had tucked in the waistband of her chaps. About twenty minutes into the ride, the woodland trail forked. "Which way?" Nancy whispered. She stopped Tristram and consulted her map. "We're in a patch of woods called Thunder Forest," she told George behind her, "but I don't see a fork on the map."

"I guess Mrs. Rogers forgot to put it on," George said.

Nancy shrugged. "The trail on her map seems to veer right, so let's go that way and see what happens."

A few minutes later, she and George heard rushing water. "We must be close to the creek," George called. Sure enough, the trail soon came to a steep bank leading down to a river about forty feet wide. *Mrs. Rogers was right,* Nancy thought. The creek was totally raging. Muddy water swirled over rocks, and the noise made it difficult for the two girls to talk.

Nancy had to shout over the rushing water. "Look to the right, George. There's a waterfall." About fifty yards away, spray shot up toward the sky where the creek crashed over a rocky cliff.

"If this is the shallow place Mrs. Rogers described, I'd hate to see what she calls deep," George said.

"It might be shallow. We just can't see the bottom because of the mud," Nancy said. "But just to be safe, let's go one at a time." Tristram hesitated at the water's edge, but Nancy urged him on. If the water was shallow like Mrs. Rogers had said, Nancy knew the horse would be strong enough to cross.

Tristram plunged in. The water splashed around his knees, and Tristram stepped carefully. "We're halfway there, boy," she told him soon, eyeing the trail on the other side.

Tristram tentatively took another step, but he slipped. Nancy grabbed his mane as Tristram's legs thrashed against the swift current. He struggled to swim forward, but it was no use. A wave of brown water crashed over a rock and swept Tristram and Nancy downstream. The spray from the falls fell on Nancy's face in a fine mist as they shot toward the precipice.

8

Hanging by a Thread

Nancy yanked the reins, hoping to head Tristram away from the falls. But no matter how hard she tried to guide him, the deep churning water pushed them forward. The roar of the falls grew louder and louder. Tristram panicked and flailed his legs as he spun in a whirlpool.

Nancy shot a look at George, who was galloping alongside her friend on the bank. George was shouting something, but her words were lost in the thunder of water crashing on rocks.

Suddenly George pointed to something ahead in the water between the riverbank and Nancy.

Nancy squinted. The spray was blurring her vision, but she forced herself to calm down and look. And then she understood. George had been trying to tell her about a rock—a flat, smooth rock that was barely higher than the water. It rose like a staircase about ten feet ahead. She tightened the reins. If she could calm Tristram she might be able to get him to climb onto it.

As she tried to guide Tristram, he resistantly pulled on his bit. The current sped around both sides of the rock, and Tristram was going with it. In seconds, they would sweep past the rock and over the falls.

Nancy stared at the rock, her eyes like lasers. She concentrated every ounce of her energy on forcing Tristram toward it. The rock was their last resort.

With his legs thrashing, Tristram stumbled onto a ledge below the water. "Good boy," Nancy breathed. "Get your footing." The ledge below the water was like a stepping-stone onto the larger rock. Nancy soothed Tristram so he could calm down and find solid ground. The horse swayed, his foothold precarious. But in moments he'd scrambled onto the ledge with all four legs.

"Steady, boy," Nancy said. She could feel his huge body shudder, and then balance itself on the underwater ledge. "Okay, now!" She slackened the reins, and Tristram surged forward. In one great leap, he bounded onto the rock.

Tristram shivered with fear as the river swirled below him. Nancy wondered if the panicky animal might bolt, plunging them both back into the water. Before Tristram had a chance to react, Nancy tightened the reins and faced him toward the creek bank where George and Derby waited tensely.

"Jump, Tristram!" Nancy commanded, slackening the reins. Tristram sprang toward the bank, barely making it as the water roiled beneath them.

"Whew!" George said, smiling with relief. "I'm so glad that rock was there."

"You and me both," Nancy said, after she'd caught her breath. "If you hadn't spotted it, Tristram and I would be over those falls by now. The rock was really hard to see since it was the same muddy brown as the water."

George shot her a wry grin. "We should have taken the left hand fork, huh?"

Nancy smiled as she turned toward the trail. "Well, George, let's go find it. The sooner we get to Mr. Bryant's fields, the better. I need to get in some sunlight, quick. I'm soaked!"

A few minutes later, they'd swung left onto the other path. It soon spilled them onto the creek bank again, but here the incline was very gradual and the river was narrower and much less turbulent. Nancy eased a quivering Tristram into the water, and the two horses had no problem fording it.

The trail continued through thick pine trees, and the girls pressed their horses into a canter. They were happy to finally reach a sunny meadow filled with butterflies. The girls lingered in the heat, and when Nancy felt drier, they galloped to the other side of the field. A farmhouse rose into view, its stone walls half hidden by ivy. Nancy and George passed through a gate into a gravel driveway overgrown with weeds. "Perfect," Nancy said. "There's no car in the driveway. Maybe Josh Bryant isn't here."

George held up crossed fingers as she gazed at the house and the nearby barn. "This place is weird," she said. "The house is a major mansion, but a bunch of its windows are broken, and the fence in the field is rotting. And look at all those birds' nests in the ivy over the front door." She pointed to the front of the house.

"Gross! I can see why Josh held a fund-raising party," Nancy said. "He could use cash to fix up this joint."

After a bit of light searching of the area surrounding the house, the girls found a section of the fence that seemed sturdy. They slid off their horses, replaced the bridles with the halters they'd brought in George's backpack, and tied Tristram and Derby to the fence with lead ropes. George also handed Nancy the silver letter opener, which Nancy placed in the back pocket of her jeans in case Mr. Bryant returned.

A small, mousy-looking girl of about fourteen

approached them from the barn. A yellow Labrador trotted next to her, wagging his tail in greeting. "Down, Duster!" the girl commanded as the dog began to jump on Nancy and George. "Where are your manners, boy?" she scolded as she gently grabbed his collar. Her gaze fell on the two girls. "Can I help you?"

"Is Mr. Bryant in?" Nancy asked.

"He's out on some errand," the girl said. "But I'm a camper here, so maybe I can help you."

"We just need to talk to Mr. Bryant," Nancy said, smiling. "How do you like camp?"

"Tomorrow is the last day, and it won't be a moment too soon," the girl said bluntly, making a face.

"What do you mean?" Nancy asked.

"This camp is the pits," the girl said. "Instead of teaching us anything useful, Mr. Bryant makes us slave away taking care of his horses. He calls the camp Happy Campers. What a joke! It's more like Labor-on-the-Cheap."

"Have you thought of coming to Green Spring next year?" George asked.

The girl's gray eyes flickered. "I heard that a bunch of weird things were happening there. Otherwise, I'd go there in a minute. See, because no one likes the camp, there are only three kids here this year—not enough to form a rally team. It's such a drag," she moaned.

"I'm sorry," Nancy said. "How did you hear about the stuff going on at Green Spring?"

The girl shrugged. "People talk. You just hear things." She checked her watch. "I'd better go muck out more stalls before Mr. Bryant comes back. He has a vicious temper." She tromped back toward the barn, and Nancy and George exchanged glances.

"This place sounds like not so much fun," George said. "We'd better check out the house before Mr. Bryant gets back. If his temper's as bad as that girl made it out to be, I don't want him to catch us trespassing."

Once inside the enormous house, Nancy and George split up to search for clues. Duster, the dog, followed Nancy. "You've found a new friend," George told Nancy on her way up the creaky stairs.

"Maybe he'll sniff up some clues," Nancy said. She followed Duster through the dining room and into the kitchen. He sat by his food bowl and pricked up his ears. "You're no help," she said, patting his head.

Turning from Duster, Nancy scanned the kitchen counters. Just as her eyes rested on an appointment book, she heard tires crunch on the gravel driveway. She hurried to the kitchen window and peered outside. A large blond man with a sour expression was climbing out of a Jeep. Mr. Bryant, Nancy guessed. She had to find a place to hide fast!

The front door slammed open, and Duster

bounded out of the room. Nancy scanned the kitchen. No closet in sight—just cabinets. *And most of the cabinets are too small to fit me,* Nancy thought. Suddenly she noticed a large cupboard with a sliding door.

Nancy climbed onto the counter and opened the cupboard door. Inside was a platform attached to a rusty cable. *A dumbwaiter,* Nancy thought—*perfect!* Hearing footsteps in the dining room, Nancy didn't waste a second. She scrambled into the dumbwaiter. Its cables creaked with her weight. Just as the steps reached the kitchen, she closed the door.

Nancy crouched in the tiny, dark space. As her eyes adjusted, she saw a thread of light coming through the crack in the door. *I hope George found a place to hide too,* Nancy thought, shifting her weight to keep her foot from falling asleep.

The dumbwaiter wobbled. The cable creaked again. Nancy held her breath. *This thing's about to go,* she realized.

Mr. Bryant hummed to himself as he puttered about the kitchen, opening cabinets, drawers, and what sounded like the refrigerator door.

A sharp crack filled Nancy's ears as a piece of the platform she sat on broke. The wood hurtled down, smacking against the basement floor. Nancy scurried back from the gaping hole.

Light flooded her eyes as the door slid open.

9

Horseplay

Mr. Bryant's face turned red with fury the moment he saw Nancy. He shot an arm into the dumbwaiter and grabbed her by the shoulders. His tiny eyes bored into her as he hauled her out.

Nancy stared at him. He was a stocky man with powerful shoulders, and greasy blond hair combed over a bald spot. She tried to think of an excuse for being in his house, but his glaring eyes made her mind go temporarily blank.

"Are ya spying on me?" he demanded.

"Uh, no, not exactly," Nancy said. She quickly fabricated a story. "See, I'm a counselor at Green Spring Farm, and Mrs. Rogers wanted me and my friend George to do her a favor—"

"I don't need any favors from Madeline Rogers," Mr. Bryant cut in.

"I said a favor *for* her," Nancy said. She felt annoyed. This guy thought the world was all about him! She dug into her back pocket and pulled out the letter opener. "We're returning this for Mrs. Rogers. She thought it might be yours. It's got your initials on it."

Mr. Bryant frowned as he took the opener and inspected it. "This is my letter opener," he admitted. "It's been missing for the past few months—ever since I held that fund-raising party."

"I found it on the floor of the tack room yesterday," Nancy explained. "Mrs. Rogers thought you might have dropped it when you came to Green Spring to pick up your horse."

"I didn't bring it to Green Spring yesterday," Mr. Bryant said. "Why would I bring it with me to pick up a horse?" He scowled at Nancy. "Is Madeline Rogers trying to play me for a fool? I'll bet she stole this letter opener from my desk at the party. After all, she was a guest there. And now her guilt is getting the better of her. She's finally returning it, but she's saying that I left it at her barn."

"It was definitely on the tack room floor," Nancy said.

Mr. Bryant reddened. "Are you contradicting me, girl? Let me remind you that you're trespassing." He turned his head suddenly and scanned the room. "You said you came over with a friend named George. Where is he? Stealing more silver?"

"George is a girl; her real name is Georgia," Nancy explained. "And she, um . . . went to find the rest room."

Mr. Bryant stared at Nancy, judging her words. He tapped the letter opener against his palm. "There's one thing I don't get about your story. If you were really here to return this opener, then why did you need to hide from me?"

Nancy glanced down, searching her brain for a good excuse. Her gaze landed on Duster. "I was hiding . . . because . . . I'm scared of your dog."

Duster wiggled up to Nancy and licked her hand.

"I want you out of my house. And your friend, too. She's been in that rest room long enough." Mr. Bryant pointed the letter opener toward the dining room. Nancy had no choice but to leave.

In the front hall, Nancy called upstairs for George. "I'm all set, George. Let's go!" she said.

"Coming!" said a muffled voice.

While waiting, Mr. Bryant prodded Nancy about how the camp season at Green Spring was going. It was clear from his tone of voice that he really didn't care.

"It's okay," Nancy lied. "And how is your camp season going?"

"Fantastically! It's a much better camp than Green

Spring, of course. Can't you tell from its name? Happy Campers. Who could resist it?" He threw up a hand, implying that anyone who chose Green Spring was an idiot.

"So your camp got its name because everyone here is happy?" Nancy asked.

"Yes indeed," he said. "And I think you're lying about Green Spring. I hear it's especially awful this summer, that it's having some, uh, problems."

"Mrs. Rogers's barn caught on fire the night before last," Nancy told him. "And someone complained to the editor of *The Horse's Mouth* that the barn wasn't up to code. Do you have any idea who would do this stuff?"

"Of course not," he barked. "Why would I? All I know is that Green Spring is way too regimented. Mrs. Rogers keeps her kids on too strict a schedule. They don't have fun because they're too busy. I think my camp is a much happier place."

George jogged down the stairs, just in time to stop Mr. Bryant from insulting Green Spring anymore. Nancy wanted to retort that the kids here didn't seem happy. How could they when he makes them do all the work? But then he'd know they'd been complaining to her, and she didn't want to get them in trouble. She shot George a look. "Let's go, George. Mr. Bryant wants us out of here."

"And don't let me see you snooping around my

farm again," he snarled, remembering his anger. He slammed the front door behind them.

Once outside, the girls untied Derby and Tristram, and replaced their halters with bridles. As they rode back to Green Spring Nancy told George about her conversation with Mr. Bryant, and how mad he was when he discovered her hiding.

When they were back at the farm, the two girls unsaddled their horses, rubbed them down, and then set them loose in a pasture. There was no sign of the campers anywhere. Nancy checked her watch. It was ten minutes to one. Lunch was probably just wrapping up.

Nancy and George hurried up to the house. Sure enough, the kids were clearing their plates and chatting about the upcoming afternoon activities. After Nancy and George had helped themselves to leftovers, Mrs. Rogers pulled them aside. "I'm so glad to see you girls," she said, "but I have some bad news. Akiyah slipped on the side of the pool when the Green Group had swimming. She bruised her left arm."

"That's awful," Nancy said. "She'll still go to the rally, though, right?"

"Yes, thank goodness," Mrs. Rogers said. "She's taking the afternoon off to rest. She'll miss cross-country practice."

"Was it an accident?" George asked. "I mean, you don't suspect sabotage or anything?"

"It definitely *wasn't* an accident," Mrs. Rogers said solemnly. "The side of the pool where she slipped was slick with oil, but no one admits to having spilled any. Someone must have spread it there on purpose."

"Let me check out the pool for clues," Nancy offered. "George, why don't you stay here and eat? You can tell Mrs. Rogers about what we did this morning."

"No problem, Nan," George said. She thrust half her turkey sandwich into Nancy's fingers. "Just do me a favor: don't let this case make you starve."

Nancy took a bite of the sandwich and grinned. "Thanks, George. I'll need every ounce of energy to figure this thing out." She walked through the tent and around the house to the pool. Whoever had mopped up the olive oil up had done an excellent job. Nancy scanned the pool for signs of it but found no traces of oil.

After thoroughly searching the pool area and finding nothing, Nancy cast her mind back to her morning at Happy Campers. *Mr. Bryant had been away from his house,* she remembered. *Had he been sneaking olive oil around Mrs. Rogers's pool?*

Nancy wandered back to the house, munching her sandwich and musing over the case so far. She felt she was stuck in a rut with her suspects and clues. Maybe a change of scene would give her a fresh perspective. She remembered that Rafael was owed a new saddle, and went back to the tent to look for Mrs. Rogers.

Nancy found the camp director talking with Elsa about Akiyah's arm. Once they'd wrapped up their conversation, Nancy said, "Why don't I take Rafael into River Heights so he can buy a new saddle? He'll need a new one for the rally, won't he?"

Mrs. Rogers beamed. "Brilliant idea, Nancy. I feel terrible about forgetting all about it. I've had way too many things on my mind lately. Please take Elsa with you. She knows exactly where Equestrian Outfitters is. And George and James can help me coach cross-country."

"A field trip!" Elsa said. "Let me round up Rafael, and we're out of here."

Forty minutes later, Nancy was parking her Mustang in front of a small shop on a side street in downtown River Heights. EQUESTRIAN OUTFITTERS appeared in black calligraphy on a sign over the door.

Nancy, Elsa, and Rafael climbed out of the car and walked into the store. Elsa and Nancy did a double take. "Bess Marvin!" Elsa said to the girl by the front counter. "I hear you got the job at *The Horse's Mouth*. Do I get a headhunter's fee?"

Bess grinned. "You'll have to take that up with Mr. Blackstone. But I warn you, he's a tough negotiator."

"What brings you here, Bess?" Nancy asked, smiling. "Business or pleasure?"

"Strictly business," Bess replied. "I'm interviewing Charlotte Neroni about the latest riding fashions. She is the owner of Equestrian Outfitters, so naturally she's an expert." Bess introduced everyone to Charlotte. She was an attractive woman in her early thirties with highlighted blond hair and a deep tan.

"So you kids are from Green Spring? Are you having fun there this summer?" she asked.

Nancy, Elsa, and Rafael nodded, not wanting to dwell on Green Spring's troubles.

"My late mother and Madeline Rogers had been best friends," Charlotte went on. "Madeline's a truly lovely woman."

"I'm just curious—do you know a man named Josh Bryant?" Nancy asked. She wanted to get as much information on Mr. Bryant as she could. If Charlotte's mother and Mrs. Rogers had been friends, Charlotte might know some of Mrs. Rogers's neighbors.

Charlotte looked confused. "That's a bit off the topic, isn't it? But I do know him. I went to a fundraiser for his camp at his house a few months ago. But I try to steer clear of him; I hear he's got a wicked temper. Why do you ask?"

"I met him at Green Spring yesterday," Nancy fudged. "And he seemed like such a grouch. So I just wondered how Mrs. Rogers puts up with him as her neighbor."

Charlotte shrugged. "At least he lives on the other side of the valley."

Within a few minutes Rafael had chosen a new saddle. After Elsa had paid the bill with Mrs. Rogers's check, the three said good-bye to Bess and Charlotte and drove back to Green Spring.

Mrs. Rogers greeted them at the barn with a compliment about Rafael's taste in saddles. "I'm happy to report that this afternoon's cross-country practice was uneventful," she told them, "except, of course, that Akiyah couldn't join us. Now, it's almost time for dinner. The theme is Italian, to celebrate our last night of camp!"

The campers ate a hearty dinner of lasagna, spaghetti, and eggplant Parmesan. When they were finished, they headed out to the barn to bed down their horses. As Nancy entered the building to help out, she bumped into Katie O'Donovan. Katie's gray eyes darted wildly, and her wavy brown hair stuck out in a messy halo around her head.

"Nancy, help me!" she begged, gripping Nancy's arm. "Someone has stolen Black Comet!"

10

A Slippery Clue

Nancy gaped at Katie. "Are you sure?" she asked.

"Yes!" Katie moaned. Her wire-rimmed glasses clouded with tears. "Nancy, I never would have quit Happy Campers if I'd known this was going to happen."

Nancy spotted George helping Cordelia lug water into her horse's stall. She motioned her over to them. "George, Black Comet is missing," she said.

George paled. "I'll get Mrs. Rogers right away. She's up at the house." George raced out the door, and Nancy turned back to Katie.

"Tell me what happened," she said.

"Well, when I got here, Black Comet wasn't in his stall, and his door to the field was wide open," Katie explained. "At first I assumed I'd spaced out and forgotten to latch it. Black Comet is smart. Without the latch, he could have pushed it open with his nose. But he wasn't outside."

"Let's go check out the field," Nancy suggested. She gave Katie a reassuring pat on the back. "Don't worry, Katie, I'm sure we'll find him."

Katie took off her glasses and wiped her eyes. Then she managed a shaky smile. "Thanks, Nancy," she said, sticking her glasses back on. "I'll try to keep calm and help you search."

Nancy led Katie into the pasture adjoining the stalls. The late summer dusk had given way to a moonlit night, and the four-acre field was twinkling with fireflies. Two horses—a dappled gray who was easy to see, and a chestnut with a white blaze on his face—were being corralled by their owners. There was no sign of any other horse. Nancy pointed to a huge oak tree down the hill. Despite the bright full moon, Nancy could see past the tree's spreading leaves.

"Black Comet's coat is so dark. Maybe he's hiding out there, and we just can't see him," Nancy said.

But a quick search proved her theory wrong. "Could he have jumped the fence?" Nancy asked. The four-and-a-half-foot fence was made of four horizontal boards painted white.

"He's capable of it," Katie replied. "But he never would."

Nancy looked around the field in every direction. "Look," she said finally, pointing to a gate at the bottom of the hill near the woods. "It's hard to see from here, but I think that gate's ajar."

Katie gasped. "Nancy, I think you're right. Now why didn't I notice?"

Nancy and Katie jogged down the hill to the open gate. On the other side, a trail opened into the woods; the same woods that separated Green Spring Farm from Happy Campers, Nancy observed.

"Whoever took Black Comet is probably riding him down that trail right now," Katie said grimly. Nancy agreed, but she didn't say anything. She didn't want to upset Katie even more.

"Nancy! Katie!" a voice called from the top of the field. The girls turned and saw Mrs. Rogers running toward them, with George and James in tow. "George told me about Black Comet, but I want to know more," Mrs. Rogers said. "Are you sure he's missing, Katie dear?"

Katie and Nancy briefed the others on what had happened. Mrs. Rogers took command of the situation. "Let's organize a search party," she said. "We'll round up some horses for the four of you to ride through the woods. Elsa and I will stay here with the kids. Oh, what a mess! I'm just grateful for the light of the full moon."

It wasn't long before Katie, Nancy, James, and

George were riding down the trail. They carried flashlights, but the bright silvery moonlight that penetrated the forest canopy was enough for them to see by.

After a few minutes, Katie spoke. "Even though we can see the trail, we can't see far through the trees. Black Comet is going to be hard to spot."

Nancy sighed. They'd be lucky if Black Comet was wandering in the woods. It was more likely that a horse thief was riding him down the trail ahead. *In that case,* she thought, *they might end up back at Happy Campers, with Josh Bryant and his famous temper greeting them.*

"Don't get discouraged yet, Katie, we've barely started our search," James said. But his voice carried a note of forced cheer.

Katie turned on her flashlight and pointed it toward the thick woods. "Black Comet!" she called. "Here, boy."

Sticks crackled deep in the woods. An owl hooted.

"Freaky," Katie whispered.

The moon passed behind a cloud, and the woods immediately darkened. Nancy turned on her flashlight to see the trail. "Hey, everyone, let's stop for a moment and listen."

As soon as the four had stopped, Nancy told Katie to call Black Comet again. But Katie's call was answered with total silence.

Once more, Katie called her horse. There was a sudden shuffle of twigs.

"Again!" George urged. This time, a faint whinny rumbled from the depths of the woods.

"Black Comet!" Katie squealed. She turned the horse she was riding toward the trees.

"Don't go in there, Katie," James warned. "You'll get lost. Let him come to you."

The whinny came again—this time, closer. "I'll go with her," Nancy said. "Black Comet's not that far away. We've got flashlights; we'll be fine."

Despite James and George's protests, Nancy led Katie off the path. In just a few moments the trees seemed to close over the trail behind them. There was nothing but unmarked woods in every direction. The trees weren't thick like evergreens, but low-hanging branches made them treacherous for horse-back riders. Nancy and Katie ducked several times to avoid getting knocked off their horses. Nancy suddenly stopped Tristram. "We shouldn't go any farther, or we'll get lost. Do you hear anything now, Katie?"

Once more, Katie called Black Comet. The girls held their breath, listening, but the woods were totally still.

Branches crackled behind them. Nancy jumped in her saddle. She turned just in time to see a large dark shape rushing toward them.

"Black Comet!" Katie cried. The white star on his face reflected in the moonlight, and announced him through the shadows. Katie quickly untied a lead rope from her waist and snapped it onto his halter. "Come on, boy. I'm not going to let you get away again." She bent over his neck and wrapped her arms around him, her face buried happily in his thick black mane.

"Okay, so we found Black Comet," Nancy said. "Now how do we get back to the trail?" The woods on all sides looked the same, dark and threatening. "George!" she called. "James! Where are you guys?"

"Here!" James and George said in unison. Nancy could tell they weren't far. She and Katie set off through the trees, stumbling toward their friends' voices. The two girls quickly reached the trail.

Katie led Black Comet beside her on the ride home. But instead of seeming cheerful, Nancy thought she seemed sad. "Is anything the matter, Katie?" Nancy asked her.

Katie said, twisted in her saddle to look at Nancy. "All these things that are happening at Green Spring are totally creeping me out. I mean, I'll finish my obligations to the rally team, but no way am I coming back next year. What happened to Black Comet is the last straw. I can't believe someone just turned him loose in the woods."

They passed through the lower gate into the

moonlit pasture. Nancy said, "You know, Katie, his disappearance may have nothing to do with all the weird stuff going on at Green Spring. He could have escaped on his own. You even said you weren't sure you'd latched his door. And someone could have left this gate open by mistake. There's no evidence that someone intentionally let him loose."

Katie rolled her eyes. "I just don't buy that, Nancy."

After putting away their horses, the four returned to the house. Mrs. Rogers was thrilled to learn their trip was a success. Nancy went straight to the kitchen for a snack of soda and cookies. On her way, Nancy passed Clare playing Monopoly with her friends in the main parlor.

Was Clare here all along? Nancy wondered, watching the four girls gossiping and giggling. Maybe. But Clare could have slipped down to the barn before dinner to set Black Comet loose. No one would have noticed.

Nancy caught Clare's gaze. Clare's gold eyes narrowed. They reminded Nancy of a tiger's, mean and proud. "Stop staring at me," Clare said coldly.

"Sorry," Nancy said. She continued toward the kitchen, but as she passed through the pantry, her eyes fell on the back stairway.

Clare's busy with her friends. Why don't I search her room again quickly? she thought.

Nancy hurried up the stairs to the third floor. Before peeking into Clare's room, she shot a glance behind her. The coast was clear.

Nancy yanked open the bottom drawer of Clare's bureau. She crossed her fingers that not all of the diary was in code. The diary was in the middle of the drawer, just where it had been yesterday. Nancy picked it up. And then she froze. Underneath the diary was a bottle of olive oil, half full.

11

Rallying toward Disaster

Nancy took the bottle out of the drawer. *Time to ask Clare a few questions,* she thought. But first, she wanted to tell Mrs. Rogers about her discovery.

She found the camp director tending to Tarzan in his pen. The monkey chattered at Nancy as he swung from a pole with his tail. "Stand back, Nancy," Mrs. Rogers warned as she took a cookie from her pocket. "Tarzan hasn't had his bedtime snack, so he's in a foul mood. When he gets like this, he's pure trouble. Though of course he knows better than to bite the hand that feeds him." She handed him the cookie.

Tarzan's manner immediately grew gentler. He was almost smiling as he gazed at it. Mrs. Rogers patted his head, then shut him in his pen as he nibbled away.

She turned to Nancy. "Something tells me you've got news."

Nancy showed her the olive oil. "I found this in Clare's drawer. I think we need to talk to her."

"Definitely," Mrs. Rogers said. "I'll get her. Let's meet in the kitchen where we can be alone."

A minute later, Mrs. Rogers and Nancy were quizzing Clare about the olive oil as they sat at the kitchen table. Several dogs lay at their feet, one in the throes of a dog dream.

Clare's face was closed and sullen. "I'm telling you, that olive oil is for my skin and hair. I take a tablespoon a day. It makes my hair much shinier." She shook back her long dark hair.

Nancy threw her a skeptical look. "Why wasn't it in the drawer when I checked yesterday?"

"Don't ask me. I didn't put it there," Clare said. "I keep it on my shelf in the bathroom. Why would I risk olive oil leaking on my stuff?"

"How much was in the bottle when you last used it?" Nancy asked.

"It was almost full," Clare said. "I bought it when I went to visit my brother the other day."

Nancy and Mrs. Rogers exchanged glances. Either Clare was lying, or someone had borrowed the oil from her bathroom shelf, poured it on the side of the pool, and then returned it to her bureau drawer. Perhaps Claire had been framed.

Nancy thought she'd try another tack. "Why was your journal written in code?" she asked.

Clare eyes flashed with anger. "Why were you snooping in my drawer, Nancy? First you find my olive oil, and now my journal? Excuse me, but my drawer is private!"

"Let me interrupt for a moment, Clare," Mrs. Rogers said. "Nancy is here to find out who is responsible for all these pranks. She's trying to keep Green Spring safe for everyone. You're a suspect because you told me that you resented my camp for its scholarship program. The quota, you said, kept you from making last year's team."

"Sure, I resented the quota, but that doesn't make me a criminal!" Clare retorted. "Anyway, I'm on this year's team, so why would I want to cause trouble for the camp?"

"Just answer Nancy's question please, Clare," Mrs. Rogers said. "Why was your journal in code?"

"So nosy people won't find out my true thoughts," Clare sputtered. She stood up. "Mrs. Rogers, I don't have to stand for this. I'm out of here."

"Sit down, Clare. You're in my house," Mrs. Rogers said, "and if I want to ask you some questions, I will. I could still remove you from the team if you don't cooperate. And if you breathe a word to anyone about Nancy's role here, your career at Green Spring is over."

"I won't tell anyone about Nancy being a snoop," Clare said. "But I'm not sitting down. I'm really tired, and I'm going to bed, whether you like it or not!" She stormed into the pantry and up the back stairs.

Mrs. Rogers sighed. "She has a point, Nancy. Why would she do all these terrible things if she's on the team this year? The more I think about it, the more convinced I am that Josh Bryant is our culprit. He was away from his house when you and George arrived this morning. He could have sneaked over here to pour that oil."

Nancy knew that Mrs. Rogers was probably right about Clare. She just wished she'd had better luck digging up clues at Mr. Bryant's. She'd have to check out his place again, threats or no threats.

The next morning there was a scramble of activity as kids and counselors prepared to leave camp. Parents showed up at ten with horse trailers in tow. After Nancy said good-bye to Juliana, her mother took Nancy aside. "Juliana has told me about all the dangerous things that have been happening here. I'm not letting her come back next year."

After Juliana had left, Nancy overheard Clare's friend Emily talking to her older sister. "It was weird at Green Spring this summer," Emily said. "All this creepy stuff kept happening, and I'm kind of relieved camp is over. I think I'm going to look for a new camp next year."

A sullen Mrs. Rogers appeared at Nancy's side. "Everywhere I turn, I hear kids saying they're not coming back," she said. "At the end of past summers, they've been upset about leaving, and can't wait until the next summer. The person who wants to shut down my camp is winning."

"Mrs. Rogers," Nancy said warmly, "I promise I'll find this person. I'm going to check Mr. Bryant's place again when I get a chance. And I'm hoping the rally will turn up more leads."

"Let's keep our fingers crossed, Nancy," Mrs. Rogers said. "We need some lucky breaks. Now, it's time to help the team get their horses ready to travel. I'm commuting back and forth from Green Spring to the fairgrounds, but the counselors and teams will stay there overnight. Elsa, James, and I will arrive at the fairgrounds early this afternoon to sign in and settle the horses. Do you think you and George could be there by dinner?"

"No problem, Mrs. Rogers. We'll see you then."

Nancy and George helped the team load their horses and equipment into trailers. They waved good-bye to Elsa and James, who were heading off to the rally in James's car. Nancy fished two sugar cubes out of her pocket. "I saved these from breakfast," she explained to George. "I think Tristram and Derby deserve a good-bye treat."

The girls fed the horses sugar and gave them big hugs. Then they climbed into Nancy's car and returned to their homes to drop off their clothes from camp and pick up fresh clothes for the rally.

The doorbell rang just after Nancy had carried her duffel bag into her front hall. In walked Bess.

"You'll never guess where I'm going," Bess announced. "To the rally!"

"That's great, Bess," Nancy said, smiling. "How'd you swing that?" She went to her room to get some clothes together, and Bess followed.

"Mr. Blackstone's sending me there to cover fashion. Stuff like what riding coat colors are hot this year."

"Awesome," Nancy said.

"And speaking of hot," Bess went on, "there's this adorable guy I met at Equestrian Outfitters. He came in to buy boots after you left. His name is Reed Fenwick, and he's on the rally team for his pony club. It's called Pine Ridge. He told me it's Green Spring's rival."

"Reed Fenwick," Nancy said slowly. "I wonder if he's related to James Fenwick. He's a counselor at Green Spring."

"James is Reed's older brother," Bess explained. "Reed doesn't seem bothered that his brother works for a rival team. Anyway, I'm excited that Reed will be at the rally too."

"I'm glad you'll be there, Bess," Nancy said. She collected her things. As the two walked out the front door, she took a moment to fill her friend in on the details of the case so far.

Nancy picked up George, and they drove to the Chatham Fairgrounds. Bess followed in her car. Once there, the three girls went immediately to dinner. Long metal tables covered with paper cloths held enough food for all six rally teams, the pony club directors, and the counselors. After pizza, salad, and ice cream, the team members left to face their first big challenge: the written test. It was held in a large room under the grandstand. Meanwhile, the counselors settled into the dorms, which they shared with all the kids. Two converted barns—one for girls, one for boys—were filled with rows of cots.

Bess sat on her cot and sorted clothes. "So is that little number hot in the horse world?" George teased, pointing to a lime green tank top that Bess was unfolding.

"It's hot anywhere," Elsa remarked, "*except* in the horse world. That color would make the calmest horse freak."

Bess shot Elsa a withering look. "James Fenwick invited me to go for a walk later, and I'm wearing this. Something tells me *he* won't freak."

"James?" Nancy echoed. "I thought the Fenwick you liked was Reed."

"It is," Bess said, "but his brother will have to do while Reed takes his test. Anyway, James is nice too. We met at dinner."

Bess quickly changed shirts and replaced her denim shorts with a white gauzy skirt and thong sandals. As she went out the door, a soft breeze blew inside, filling the dorm with the smell of horses and honeysuckle. "It's a beautiful night," Nancy told Elsa and George. "I'm going for a walk too, to explore the fairgrounds."

Ten minutes later, Nancy was wandering through a group of barns where the horses were kept. She headed toward the grandstand, which overlooked the racetrack. A light shone through some windows looking into the room in which the riders were taking their test. The night was clear, and from the bleachers she could see the amusement park at the far left of the track. The lights on the Ferris wheel glittered and danced. To the right of the track were a few farms, some dense woods, and fields where the cross-country event would be held.

Nancy climbed down from the grandstand and began to walk toward the amusement park. It looked like it was about half a mile away. A few feet away from the grandstand, a couple leaned over the racetrack fence. Nancy instantly recognized the figures as Bess and James. She moved away, not wanting to disturb them—but before she left, she overheard a fragment of their conversation.

"Do you feel competitive with Reed because you guys are on different teams?" Bess was asking.

"Not really. It's okay if Green Spring loses. I'll just root for Pine Ridge, since that's Reed's team," James replied.

Nancy slipped away, turning James's words over in her mind. He seemed perfectly cool about the prospect of Green Spring losing. She wondered if he could have anything to do with the sabotage. What if James was hurting Green Spring to give Reed a better chance of winning?

Nancy chewed her lip. She felt frustrated by the lack of clues and suspects. James was a long shot, she knew. Closing down Green Spring was an extreme way to give your brother an edge. Still, it couldn't hurt to check him out for clues. The boys' dorm was way too crowded at this time of night to search, but what about James's car?

Nancy headed toward the small parking lot in front of barn 5, where the Green Spring horses were stabled. She spotted James's silver Honda two cars down from her Mustang.

Please be unlocked, Nancy thought as she tried the

driver's door. To her relief, it clicked open. She climbed into the car and began to search. Tattered maps and wrappers from fast-food restaurants littered the floor and seats. Suddenly Nancy felt something lumpy under a paper bag. She tossed the bag aside, and caught her breath. A bar of white soap gleamed in the lamplight from the window.

Nancy picked up the soap and inspected it. Its edges were dull and scratched.

12

Terror at Dressage

Nancy replaced the soap and covered it with the bag. Nothing else in the car looked suspicious, so she climbed out and shut the door. As she headed back to the girls' dorm, Bess appeared from the opposite direction.

"How was your walk with James?" Nancy asked.

"Fun," Bess said. "And when we ran into Reed coming out of the test, the night got even better."

Nancy laughed. "Are you paying attention to what the Fenwicks are wearing? Your column covers boys' clothes, too, right?"

"Uh-huh, but the jeans they wore tonight won't make an interesting story. I'll have to pay extra attention to Reed's riding outfits." She shot Nancy a coy smile. "Just doing my job."

"Where are the Fenwicks now?" Nancy asked, looking around.

"In the boys' dorm," Bess replied. "The teams have to get up early tomorrow for dressage."

Nancy lowered her voice and told Bess about finding the bar of soap in James's car. "I don't know . . . soap is just a weird thing to have on the floor of your car," she finished. "And the corners were scraped, like . . . well, someone might have written with it."

"Do you really suspect James?" Bess asked, wide-eyed.

"Let's just say I've added him to my list of suspects," Nancy said. "He's been at Green Spring all along, and he has a motive: getting Reed's team to win."

"I can't believe James would go to that much trouble just to improve Reed's chances of winning," Bess said. "Plus, Clare's been at Green Spring all along too. And don't forget Mr. Bryant. Even though he wasn't staying at the camp like Clare and James, his letter opener was near Rafael's saddle. That's pretty incriminating."

"But why would Clare want to harm Green Spring when she's on the team?" Nancy asked.

Bess shrugged. "I don't know. Still, the soap proves nothing about James. It's like Clare and her olive oil—no proof. Josh Bryant is much more likely."

"Bess, I'll make a deal with you," Nancy said. "If nothing bad happens at the rally, I'll stop suspecting

James, and focus on Josh. After all, James is here, and Josh isn't."

"Makes sense," Bess agreed. "Now let's get our beauty sleep, Nan. I have to wake up early to cover the latest fashions in dressage!"

At breakfast the next morning, Mrs. Rogers gave her team a brief pep talk, then everyone headed for the Green Spring stables to prepare the horses for the morning event.

As stable manager, Cordelia Zukerman gave the other four team members advice on bathing and grooming the horses, and cleaning their tack. She made sure the stalls were always clean, and that feeding went according to schedule. From time to time, judges would roam the stables, evaluating each team's stable management skills.

"Cordelia, you're great at organizing us," Katie pronounced as Cordelia helped her polish stirrups.

"Could you help me brush Dido's tail please, Cordelia?" Akiyah asked, looking frustrated as her mare swished her tail at flies.

"How do I tie my stock?" Rafael asked. He was already dressed in formal dressage wear: a black riding coat, ivory-colored breeches, black boots, and a black derby hat. In front of a makeshift mirror in the tack room, he struggled with his stock, which resembled a large white tie.

"Dressage clothes look totally Victorian," Nancy told George in a low voice. "I mean, what news is there for Bess to cover if the style never changes?"

George shrugged. "Maybe the sock colors change each decade?"

"Well, even if the fashion hasn't changed since the eighteen hundreds, the clothes are kind of cool to look at," Nancy said, watching Rafael secure his tie with a large gold pin.

Mrs. Rogers bustled into the tack room. "Hey kids, why are you dressing so soon? Green Spring's round isn't scheduled until eleven. You'll get horse hairs all over your beautiful clothes!"

"No, we won't," Clare protested. "Our horses are squeaky clean. General Cordelia has made sure of that. Still, I think you guys are stupid to get dressed now. It's only ten."

Akiyah rolled her eyes. Leaning toward Nancy and George, she whispered, "Clare's being especially bad these days because none of her friends are here to distract her."

James called the other counselors over. "Why don't we go over to the dressage ring now and watch the other teams? I don't want to get in Cordelia's way."

The counselors told their team they'd see them later, then set off through the cluster of barns for the ring. As they walked, Nancy observed various rally

108

teams tending to their horses. The morning light bounced off a variety of sizes and colors of horses. Newly brushed coats gleamed like satin. A beautiful chestnut mare, her coat a coppery brown, waited patiently while her owner combed her mane. A bright yellow palomino gelding stood next to her, swishing flies with his long white tail.

The counselors arrived at the dressage ring, which was in a grassy meadow near the amusement park. Bess was at the side of the ring, jotting down notes. Parents, counselors, and pony clubbers made up the rest of the audience.

A judge sat in a folding chair at the end of the ring by the letter C. He was studying a rider on a frisky bay.

Nancy did a double take. The judge looked familiar. She moved closer. There was no doubt about it— she'd know Josh Bryant anywhere. His pudgy frame overhung the flimsy chair, and his blond hair looked even greasier than it did.

"Do you see what I see?" George asked Nancy, appearing at her side.

"I wonder if Mrs. Rogers knows he's here," Nancy said. "I'm amazed he's qualified to be a judge."

The Green Spring team trotted up to the ring. "Hey, you guys look sharp," Elsa told them as the other counselors and Mrs. Rogers clustered around. The four riders looked terrific, Nancy thought, in their black habits and derbies. And their horses looked striking, too, all clean and brushed.

"Good luck, guys," James said, smiling. "We're all rooting for you."

Nancy took Mrs. Rogers aside and asked if she realized that Mr. Bryant was judging. With her hand shading her eyes, Mrs. Rogers looked toward the end of the ring. "I was hoping he wouldn't be here," she said. "But I'm not surprised. Josh has been judging events for years. Since he doesn't have a team entered, he's considered impartial. Of course, you and I know he's not."

The team scheduled before Green Spring finished, and everyone clapped. "Whoops, I'd better go wish Rafael luck," Mrs. Rogers said. "He's up first."

A couple minutes later, an announcer said, "The Green Spring Pony Club! Rafael Estevez, on Clown." Rafael walked Clown into the ring and saluted to Mr. Bryant. He expertly took the dappled gray horse through the intricate dressage paces. After a perfect round he left the ring, to the sound of polite applause. Katie followed on Black Comet. Mr. Bryant scowled as he watched his former pupil, but Nancy could tell the audience was impressed.

Clare went next, with Akiyah standing by. After saluting Mr. Bryant, Clare guided Victoria in tight circles of walks and trots. Victoria chomped at the bit, tossing her head nervously. "Settle down, girl,"

Clare whispered as she trotted by Nancy and George. But Victoria wasn't listening. Her mouth was foaming, and her eyes rolled.

"That mare is so skittish," Mrs. Rogers murmured. "She's the reason Clare didn't make last year's team. I thought she seemed calmer this year. Boy, did I misjudge that."

Clare urged Victoria into a perfectly controlled canter down the side of the ring. "Clare's a good rider, though," Elsa declared. "I'll think she'll pull this off."

A loud explosion suddenly shook the air. Smoke spewed from a clump of bushes next to Mr. Bryant's chair. Everyone jumped.

Victoria neighed in terror. Rearing up, she sprang forward and bolted through the ring. The audience screamed as the mare crashed through the short picket fence.

Clare yanked the reins, desperately trying to keep Victoria in the unpopulated field away from the fair rides. But it was no use. Victoria was uncontrollable. She raced into the amusement park area, and narrowly skirted the roller coaster. A cry rose from the crowd as she galloped straight for the merry-go-round.

"Turn her, Clare," Mrs. Rogers shouted, "or she'll trample all those kids!"

13

Cross-Country Craziness

Nancy froze, staring in horror at the runaway horse. Clare had to stop Victoria fast, or crowds of people would be injured. Kids and parents scattered in panic as the horse raced toward them. Clare leaned back in the saddle, jabbing the reins, straining to control Victoria. Screams overwhelmed the jolly music of the carousel.

Clare yanked the reins hard to the right in a last-ditch effort to avoid the carousel. Nancy held her breath. Finally, Victoria was turning—just four feet from the ride.

Shortening the reins, Clare forced control of the terrified animal. While kids cried in their parents' arms, still afraid of being trampled, Clare guided Victoria to an empty patch of grass.

Mrs. Rogers ran off to help Clare. George, Elsa, and James followed, but Nancy stayed behind. She wanted to see what had caused the explosion. Nancy hurried to the bushes and began poking around. Pieces of burned paper littered the ground. Nearby, the charred remains of a small firecracker told her what had happened. *One thing's for sure,* Nancy thought as she picked up the firecracker, *Clare couldn't have lit this—and she wouldn't have scared her own horse.*

Nancy shot a look at the judge's chair, which was now empty. Mr. Bryant was already returning to the dressage ring, though. Nancy studied him ambling across the lawn. His chair had been next to the bushes. *Could he have lit the firecracker and then tossed it in? Maybe,* she thought. The bushes were so close that he could have gotten away with it. James had also been around here, but Nancy couldn't remember exactly where he'd stood before the explosion.

Mr. Bryant scowled at Nancy. "Whatcha looking at, young lady?" he snapped.

"Did you see anyone hanging around these bushes?" Nancy asked.

"How could I have? I was watching the contestants' every move. You should tell that girl to control her horse better. She could have caused a mess out there."

He dropped back down on his chair, breathing

hard from his trip across the lawn. Nancy showed him the firecracker, and he summoned a rally official on his walkie-talkie. A few minutes later, everyone else returned to the ring. After the official made sure the ring was safe, Clare was allowed to try again.

While Clare was taking Victoria through her paces, Nancy spoke to Mrs. Rogers. "I'm hoping that firecracker was random, but I'm afraid the trouble-maker has followed us here from Green Spring."

"I'm worried too, Nancy," Mrs. Rogers said. "We could pretend that the firecracker was a random occur-rence, but my gut tells me it's part of the pattern."

This time, Clare's round was almost perfect. Akiyah and Dido were next, and they were very pleased with their results. When Green Spring had finished, Mr. Bryant stood up for lunch.

Back at the stable, the Green Spring team rubbed down their horses and returned them to their stalls. After Cordelia made sure that everything looked shipshape, the team members hurried to lunch. While munching on her grilled cheese sandwich, Nancy kept an eye on James—but nothing about him suggested anything the least bit suspicious. He chatted with everyone: the counselors, the team, and Mrs. Rogers. And he seemed completely at ease.

"Hey guys, we've got the afternoon off," Elsa announced. "Other teams are scheduled for dressage this afternoon. Let's have some fun!"

"Not so fast," Cordelia said. "Maybe you counselors can hang out, but the team has work to do. Tomorrow is the cross-country event. The route's being posted this afternoon, and we've got to study it."

The team members groaned. "You're such a drag, Cordelia," Clare said, pouting. "Always making us work."

"That's why we're going to win this rally," Akiyah said firmly.

After lunch, the team congregated at rally head-quarters off the dining hall to study the cross-country map. James offered to stay with the kids to help plan their rides, while Elsa and George went to play tennis at some nearby courts. Nancy headed back to the dressage ring; she wanted to make sure Mr. Bryant was still there, judging the event as he should be.

Sure enough, he was sitting in the same chair, jotting down notes on the rider in the ring. Nancy watched the dressage with Bess for a while, then returned to her dorm to read and think about the case. She was sure the firecracker had been lit by whoever had played the other pranks. She just wished she had more leads.

The rest of the afternoon was uneventful. That evening, a buzz of excitement filled the air as the teams looked forward to competing cross-country the next day. Hands down, it was everyone's favorite event. The order of the teams was posted at dinner. Green Spring was scheduled to go first, at nine A.M. sharp.

The day dawned beautifully. After a breakfast of waffles and fruit, the Green Spring team gathered in their section of the stables to brush and feed their horses. Bess showed up, too, pad and pencil in hand, angling for an interview. "I know the attire for cross-country is less formal than dressage or stadium jumping," she said to the team. "Are there any new looks for this year?"

"Are you kidding?" Akiyah exclaimed. "Cross-country is the only cool event when it comes to clothes. We wear Polo shirts in lots of bright colors, and our horses get to wear colorful saddle pads. We also wear back protectors for safety."

"Bor-ing!" Clare complained. "I'd like to make bikini tops the dress code. They'd make a lot more sense in this heat."

Katie grinned. "And win us points with the judges."

"If you want to know the hip color this year, Bess," Akiyah said, "it's magenta. That's what *I'm* wearing."

Cordelia rushed over with Katie's saddle, and a lime green pad. "No time to gab, girls. Let's move. It's already eight thirty, and the horses aren't even tacked up."

The Green Spring counselors gathered early by

the entrance to the cross-country course. They'd offered to stand at different places along the so they could jump in if there was an emergency at any time. Elsa explained to Nancy and George that the course ran over two miles of countryside, and each rider had five and a half minutes to complete it. Judges stood by each of fourteen jumps that had been positioned around woods, valleys, fields, and streams. Red flags on poles were placed at certain points to guide the riders in the right direction. The jumps were identified with white flags and numbers.

A rally official drove the volunteers to their places in a Jeep, and handed them walkie-talkies. Nancy was asked to stand near a log jump—jump number 7—set directly in front of a clear, babbling stream in a little valley. A judge sat in a canvas chair by the jump, in the shade of an oak tree.

Nancy felt sorry for the riders since they had to wear long-sleeved Polo shirts and back protectors. She already felt hot in her pink T-shirt and khaki shorts. *At least the day was sunny,* she thought. She could just make out the next jump in the valley below the stream. It was an imitation chicken coop. Josh Bryant was the judge. A white flag with a black number 8 flapped in the breeze on one side.

Mr. Bryant glared at Nancy, but she was too far away to hear whatever obnoxious comments he might make.

At least I can keep an eye on him today, she thought.

Nancy checked her watch. It was nine fifteen. The first Green Spring rider should be coming soon.

A faint sound of galloping hooves grew louder and louder until Akiyah and Dido appeared on the crest of the hill. Akiyah's eyes were totally focused on the next jump as she urged Dido toward the log fence. *Go!* Nancy thought. With Akiyah hunched low over the mare's mane, Dido sailed over the jump effortlessly. She splashed through the stream, then climbed up a small incline that opened into a huge field.

Nancy took her eyes off Akiyah for a moment to glance at the judge. A thrill went through her as she watched the judge mark Akiyah's score. It was a perfect zero—meaning no penalties!

Dido raced through the field, with Akiyah guiding her around the flag that pointed toward Mr. Bryant's chicken coop. But as Dido turned, she suddenly lost her footing.

Nancy stared in astonishment as Dido slipped and stumbled. The mare could barely lift her legs. Akiyah urged her on, but she came to a standstill in front of the fence as if she were stuck in putty.

What's going on? Nancy wondered. She crossed the stream and ran down the hill. "Akiyah!" Nancy shouted. "What's wrong?"

Akiyah twisted in her saddle. "Dido's in a marsh.

She can't get enough traction to make the jump. Be careful, Nancy. You don't want to get stuck too."

"I won't," Nancy said, but already her sneakers were squelching in the wet grass. "Here, throw me the reins and I'll lead you to firmer ground."

Akiyah tossed Nancy the reins, and Nancy tugged. Stretching her neck toward Nancy, Dido lifted one hoof, then another, out of the swampy ground. Strange suction noises came with every step.

"Go, girl," Akiyah urged, squeezing her knees against the saddle. With Nancy and Akiyah's encouragement, Dido slogged her way out of the marsh and on to dry ground.

"Excellent!" Akiyah said, taking back the reins. "Now, what kind of person would put a jump in a marsh?"

"Do you have your map?" Nancy asked her.

Akiyah pulled her route map out of her pocket and held it so Nancy could see it too. The girls exchanged puzzled looks. "The flags must be wrong, Nancy. This jump isn't on the course," Akiyah said.

Nancy looked at the map again. Instead of veering right toward the chicken coop, the route headed left to the top of the hill. The next jump, number 8, was a post-and-rail on the other side.

Nancy called to Mr. Bryant, who was sitting by the jump about twenty feet away. It was very suspicious, she thought, that the messed-up jump was his.

"Come over here!" he shouted back unpleasantly.

"How lazy can that guy be?" Akiyah whispered. "He can't even be bothered to get out of his chair to help us!"

The girls went over to him. After studying Akiyah's map, Mr. Bryant said, "I admit this is odd, girls. I have no idea how or why those flags were rerouted."

"Did you notice anything weird when you got here this morning—like a person hanging around?" Nancy asked.

"Nope. You know, anyone could have switched the flags before the day began," he said. "Either last night or first thing this morning."

"How do you think the person got out here?" Nancy asked. "It's far from the fairgrounds."

He shrugged. "Don't ask me. A rally official drove all the judges to their fences. We just followed the flags. Whoever switched them must have done it before eight thirty this morning when we arrived."

Nancy studied him, measuring his sincerity. He stared back as if daring her to contradict him. *Sure, anyone could have switched the flags,* she thought, *and "anyone" includes* you.

Nancy scanned the area around the flags for clues. On the ground by the white jump flag, something caught her eye: something gold, glinting in the sun. She reached down and loosened it from the mud. A woman's bangle bracelet. But whose?

14

Monkey Business

A bracelet? Nancy thought. *Maybe Clare's . . .*

Nancy stood up and looked over at Akiyah and Mr. Bryant, who were studying the map again. She showed them the bracelet. "Do either of you recognize this?" she asked.

They shook their heads, then focused back on the map.

Nancy slipped the bracelet into her pocket, happy to have a clue. There was a chance the bracelet didn't belong to the person who had switched the flag, but it probably did. After all, Akiyah was the first person to ride the course, and the bracelet wasn't hers.

Nancy called rally headquarters on her walkie-talkie and explained the switched flag. After a brief investigation by a rally official, the flag was placed at its proper jump, Mr. Bryant was relocated, and Akiyah was allowed to start again.

The rest of Green Spring's run went smoothly. Each rider cleared the log fence perfectly. Not all the teams were so skilled, and Pine Ridge suffered a setback when Reed Fenwick's horse tapped the fence with his hind foot.

Even with her team's success, Nancy felt frustrated. Her duties required her to be on the course all day. She'd have to wait until later to investigate the case.

Every now and then she felt the bracelet in her pocket through the fabric of her shorts. Whose could it be? Clare wore several bangle bracelets, both gold and silver, but Nancy couldn't remember if she owned one like this. The shadows began to lengthen over the hills as the final team completed its round. Nancy knew where Josh Bryant had been all day, but what about Clare and James? They'd had the whole afternoon to plan more tricks.

After the event finished, judges and volunteers returned to the stables. Nancy found Clare giving Victoria a bath. She showed her the bracelet and asked if it was hers.

"No way," Clare said, sounding insulted. "I wouldn't buy a bracelet like that. It's too plain—like something my mom might wear."

Nancy turned to James, who was holding Victoria.

"Have you noticed anyone wearing this?" she asked.

James shrugged. "Can't help you, Nancy. But I'm not really tuned in to jewelry. If someone wore this in front of me all day, I still might not recognize it."

At dinner, Nancy kept a close watch on Clare and James, as well as on Mr. Bryant, who ate at a table reserved for judges. No matter how hard she studied them, though, she couldn't detect any suspicious behavior.

In the middle of dinner, Rafael said, "It all makes me nervous—that firecracker yesterday, and today, the misplaced flag. I wonder what's going to get us tomorrow."

"Don't say that, Rafael," Katie exclaimed. "You're scaring me."

"Me too," Cordelia said. "I'm not even sure it's worth being at the rally, knowing someone is trying to hurt us."

"Cordelia the 'iron lady' is feeling down?" Akiyah teased. "Things must be *really* bad!"

Nancy wanted to lift the team's mood. She decided to give them a pep talk. "Guys, you're doing great at the rally," she said, forcing a smile. "Your scores are awesome; you and Pine Ridge have the lowest so far! If you ace the stadium jumping tomorrow, then you're the winners. So don't let the firecracker or flag get you down. Just make it through one more day."

"But what if we win?" Katie asked, slumping her shoulders. "Our reward will be that we'll go to the national rally, and the person will probably show up there. This torture might go on for days!"

Nancy sighed. What Katie said was true. If they won the rally tomorrow, they'd go on to the nationals. And who knew whether these problems would just continue there?

While the rally teams went to bed down their horses, Nancy, Bess, and George took a walk so they could talk about the case. The three headed over to the amusement park to get some cotton candy.

"I have to solve the case by tomorrow," Nancy declared as she picked a piece of the pink fluff off the white paper holder. It melted in her mouth. "Unless, of course, we win. Then I'll have until the end of Nationals to solve it."

"Why can't you keep working on it after the rally ends?" Bess asked.

"Because without the camp or rally going on, the person will go into hiding," Nancy explained. "There won't be anything or anyone for him or her to hurt. Green Spring's reputation will be greatly affected by what happened this summer. We need to show that Green Spring's safe, so people will want to come back."

"It's true," George said gravely. "You should have heard the kids talk as they were leaving camp, Bess. They were totally weirded out. No one wanted to set foot at Green Spring Farm again. And all the strange things that happened here at the rally are just making things worse."

"So the only way to fix Green Spring's reputation is to catch this person and show everyone there's no more danger," Bess said. "Poor Mrs. Rogers. Her pony club is such a source of happiness for her. What would she do if she had to close it down?"

"I can't imagine her retiring," George said. "She's the type who has to keep busy with a project she loves. Without Green Spring, she'd be miserable."

"The thing that gets me about this case is the lack of leads," Nancy said. "Just when I rule out Clare, I find a bracelet. And just when I suspect Josh the most, he's stuck in a chair all day doing nothing wrong. And James's motive is weak."

"Now you're talking," Bess said. "James is definitely not guilty."

"Is that what he told you on one of your walks?" George joked.

"I just know it," Bess proclaimed, "thanks to my trusty sixth sense!"

"Those jumps look terrifying!" Bess said the following afternoon. Twelve brightly colored jumps formed a tight course inside the stadium jumping ring, which had been set up on the racetrack. Bess, Nancy, and George sat in the front bleacher of the grandstand with parents, counselors, and pony clubbers who'd completed their rounds that morning.

Green Spring was the first to go after lunch. Elsa, James, Mrs. Rogers, and Cordelia were prepping the riders at the front gate of the ring.

"The jumps are supposed to be scary," George told Bess. "Only the bravest horses and best riders do well in this event. It's a huge challenge."

"I've heard it's the hardest of the three events," Nancy said. "The horses have to make perfect rounds in just a couple of minutes without so much as nicking a fence. Refusals earn big penalties."

"Speaking of challenges," Bess said, "have you had any breaks in the case since last night?"

"Nope," Nancy said. "Things were quiet this morning, but Green Spring wasn't competing. It's our turn now, and I'm worried. I told Cordelia to pay extra attention to the saddle and bridle straps, and I just finished checking the grandstand and track for stuff like firecrackers and booby traps."

With the blow of a whistle, Rafael and Clown appeared in the ring. Bess flipped open her notebook and began taking notes, while Nancy and George fixed their eyes on Rafael.

After saluting Mr. Bryant in the judge's chair, Rafael made Clown trot in a tight circle at the top of the ring to warm up for his run. Once he was ready, he urged him into a canter, and headed into the first jump: A large board painted with multicolored butterflies. Clown sailed over it. The next jump was an imitation hedge painted electric green, and once again Clown cleared it. On and on Clown went, gracefully springing over the fences, each one brighter and more outlandish than the one before.

As Clown jumped the next to last fence with no problem, Nancy's heart beat faster. He was almost done—and nothing had happened! The last jump loomed ahead.

The fence was made up of two huge barrels lying on their sides, each one painted red, yellow, and green. They were topped by red, yellow, and green striped poles. It stood right across the ring from Nancy, George, and Bess.

Clown hesitated at the bizarre-looking fence, but Rafael confidently pressed him forward. Just as Clown reared up to jump, there was a commotion— from inside one of the barrels!

A brown furry creature swung out of the barrel and onto the pole. Nancy gaped. It was Tarzan, Mrs. Rogers's monkey. He screamed in surprise when he saw the airborne horse.

But Clown was even more surprised. The instant he saw Tarzan, he swerved toward the side of the ring, hooves flailing and nostrils flaring. Nancy froze as the huge animal loomed over her.

"Run," Bess shouted, "or we'll get crushed!"

15

Mirror, Mirror

Bess's notebook flew into the air as everyone scattered. Spectators screamed as Clown knocked through the barrel fence, then crashed against the side of the ring. A sickening crack filled the air. Clown was about to thunder into the grandstand.

Nancy scrambled onto the higher bleachers with Bess and George. She held her breath, watching the frantic horse sideswipe the fence.

Clown reared again, but this time away from the fence. Nancy exhaled with relief. The fence had bent from his weight, but the boards hadn't totally broken.

Clown bolted for the middle of the ring, and Rafael tightened the reins. Even though Nancy could hardly hear him, she could tell by his facial expression that he was soothing Clown.

Finally, Clown stopped by the butterfly jump. Rafael leaped off, and began inspecting his horse for injuries. The terrified animal tossed his head, sending flecks of foam into the air.

Mrs. Rogers and a man with a black bag ran into the ring to check Clown. Nancy guessed the man was a vet.

A sudden cry went up in the grandstand. "Catch him!" came a child's high-pitched voice. Nancy turned to see Tarzan leaping gleefully around the bleachers, trailing a leash. A group of kids was following him. Every time someone almost caught him, though, he skipped out of the way, chattering and teasing.

"That creature is like Curious George," Bess commented. "He's really mischievous."

"You're telling me," Nancy said. "He belongs to Mrs. Rogers. I wonder how he got from her house to that barrel."

"Got him!" a girl cried, holding up his leash. "Whoops!" she added as the monkey sprang at her. She dropped the leash the moment he bared his teeth.

"Allow me," George said. She dashed up the stairs three at a time and grabbed the leash. "Chill out!" she told Tarzan sternly. "No more monkeying around for you."

Tarzan obeyed, though his expression was sly. Elsa met George on her way down and took the leash from her. "Mrs. Rogers wants me to lock him in the stable until she drives home," Elsa said. "She can't figure out how Tarzan got here. Someone must have stolen him out of her house this morning. That's the last time she saw him."

"This is too weird," Nancy said, joining her. She glanced at the ring, where officials were checking for booby traps. One official pulled a banana peel and a dish of water from the barrel. "Someone must have put food and water inside that barrel for Tarzan so he'd stay put," Nancy added, "and then the sound of Clown's hooves scared him out."

"But who would do something like that?" Bess wondered. "It's mean to the animals, as well as to Rafael."

"It's terrible," Elsa agreed. "I think this is the last straw for a lot of Green Spring kids. I hope Mrs. Rogers will have enough takers for her camp next summer—but I wouldn't count on it."

"Think of all that scholarship money going to waste," Nancy said. "I wish I knew why this person is so desperate to shut Green Spring down. The program is great."

While Elsa hurried off with Tarzan, Nancy shot a look at Mr. Bryant. He was sitting in an umpire's chair at the far end of the ring. The judge had been there every moment of the day, except lunch. She turned toward the Green Spring team, huddled on their horses by the gate. James and Cordelia were standing by the riders. They were watching the officials who were inspecting the ring.

All her suspects—James, Clare, and Josh Bryant—were in plain sight, looking innocent and unconcerned. But Nancy knew that any one of them could have brought Tarzan into the ring while it was empty during lunch. Of course, Mr. Bryant would have been on a very tight schedule if he had to drive to Mrs. Rogers's house and back to fetch Tarzan. Clare and James, on the other hand, had the whole morning off.

Mr. Bryant announced that Rafael could take his turn again. This time, Clown had a perfect round. Akiyah, Katie, and Clare followed him, and they also scored perfectly. Nancy, Bess, and George hurried over to the gate.

"Congratulations, guys!" Nancy said, smiling. "You didn't make one mistake."

"I bet you won," Bess declared.

Mrs. Rogers grinned. "I bet you're right. But we won't know for sure until the last three teams perform this afternoon. Green Spring's scores on cross-country, stadium jumping, and the written test are perfect. But a couple of our dressage scores show penalties. So we'll just have to bite our fingernails until we learn the final results."

"And if you win, it's on to Virginia!" Bess said.

"I sure hope so," Mrs. Rogers said fervently. "I

also hope that whoever is plaguing us with these dangerous pranks gets caught by then. The last thing we need is for him to show up in Virginia."

After a solemn pause, Cordelia said, "Okay, everyone, let's get the horses sponged off and walked. They deserve a nice long rest after their awesome performances here."

The counselors offered to come back to the stables and help. Bess turned back toward the seats. "I'm staying here, guys," she said. "Pine Ridge is up next, and they're supposed to have cool stadium jumping coats." She flashed a smile at James. "Or so Reed told me the other night."

James looked puzzled. "His coat is gray. How cool is that?"

"Hmm," Bess said playfully, "I'll give him a break and call it 'soft silver' in my article."

After waving good-bye to Bess, the counselors followed the team. On the way to the stable, they passed some food concession stands, and the smell of burgers, hot dogs, and french fries filled the air. James stopped for a second and took in the smell. "I'm hungry, and that smell is totally tempting. I'm stopping here for a cheeseburger. Don't wait for me, guys. I'll be back soon."

He veered toward a stand on the right and paused in front of it. Nancy eyed him. *Hungry?* she thought. *But we just had lunch less than an hour ago. Maybe*

James has a big appetite. Or maybe he has something he needs to do without the rest of us hovering over his shoulder. . . .

"I'm checking out his story," Nancy whispered to George. She slipped away from the rest of the group.

From behind a ticket kiosk, Nancy watched James linger by the burger stand until the team was out of sight. He then glanced furtively from side to side and hurried away without any food. Nancy followed him.

Picking up his pace, James headed toward the far side of the racetrack. Nancy was careful to keep at least thirty feet between them. Now and then, James would stop and look over his shoulder—but Nancy was quick. Each time he stopped, she'd slip into a crowd or behind a fence post before he could see her.

A racehorse starting gate stood at the edge of the track. James was jogging straight for it, putting too much distance between them. Nancy had to catch up, or she might lose him!

Nancy followed him onto the track. Once there, she broke into a quiet run. Her sneakers had no traction in the soft turf, though, so she could move only so fast. It was like having your legs paralyzed in a nightmare, she thought. She only hoped James didn't turn around. Besides a few scattered fence posts, there were no places to hide on the open track.

James was almost at the gate. A woman popped up from one of the stalls and waved to him.

Nancy scurried behind a fence post. *Did she see me?* Nancy wondered. Even from her distance of a hundred feet, the woman looked familiar. She was slender and attractive, with chin-length highlighted blond hair.

Nancy suddenly recalled the face. The woman was Charlotte Neroni, owner of Equestrian Outfitters—the store she and Rafael had gone to to buy his new saddle. Nancy remembered that she was the daughter of Mrs. Rogers's best friend, Eleanor Neroni, who had died a few years ago. But how were Charlotte and James connected?

Nancy scurried from post to post, trying to get close enough to hear their conversation. But before she could get to a good place, James suddenly hurried away. He was carrying a white legal-size envelope.

Nancy hunched down behind a post, hoping he wouldn't see her as he passed by. Nancy's gaze followed James as he jogged back the way he'd come. Nancy wondered what was in the envelope.

Nancy's curiosity shifted from James to Charlotte. Was Charlotte paying James to sabotage Green Spring? The envelope looked like it might contain money. Or maybe it held some sort of document. If she *was* paying him to hurt Green Spring, the big question, of course, was why.

Nancy followed James with her eyes before he blended into the crowd. *I can always catch up with him later,* she thought. Nancy quickly looked back at Charlotte. Her heart skipped a beat. The woman was already hurrying away from the starting gate, in the direction of the amusement park. In a minute, Nancy would lose sight of her.

Nancy slipped out from behind her post and jogged after Charlotte, but Charlotte had picked up her pace. As Charlotte approached the rides, the crowds thickened. Nancy could hardly see her.

I've got to run faster, Nancy thought. She broke into a sprint, dodging clusters of people, ticket kiosks, and hot dog stands. Nancy's spirits lifted as she caught sight of Charlotte's blond head bobbing in the crowd just ahead.

Charlotte stopped and looked around, as if deciding which way to go. She glanced over her shoulder, and her eyes flickered. *She knows I'm following her,* Nancy realized.

Charlotte froze, like a deer about to run. "Wait!" Nancy yelled. "I just want to ask you a few questions."

But Charlotte didn't waste another second. She sprang forward, frantically making for the carnival rides. Nancy increased her pace, barely keeping Charlotte in sight as she zigzagged through the crowds.

As Nancy ran through the carnival, she passed tiny kids holding huge clouds of cotton candy; green-haired teenagers throwing darts at balloons; and lines for rides snaking across the open spaces. Nancy almost collided with a child carrying a slice of pizza and a huge glass of soda. But in spite of all the obstacles, she kept track of Charlotte.

Suddenly a kid carrying a stuffed bear blocked Nancy's way. Nancy hopped to the side, trying to avoid him, but the kid spun around in front of her again. Tears trickled down his face as he stared up at her. "I'm sorry," she said. "Did I hurt you?"

"Where's Mommy?" he wailed.

"I don't know," Nancy said, her heart sinking as Charlotte's frosted head slipped out of sight. "Weren't you with her?"

A woman grabbed the boy's hand and yanked him toward her. "I told you not to wander off, Eric," she scolded. "Mommy got worried."

Nancy took off. Where was Charlotte? She pivoted in every direction, searching the crowds, but there was no sign of her. *Don't tell me I've lost her—I was so close!* Nancy thought.

Frustrated, Nancy scanned the area again. More and more people poured into the park. Lines to the most popular rides—the scrambler, the roller coaster, and the whirligig—lengthened by the second.

Nancy froze. Something familiar had just passed by her. But where did it go, and what was it? She looked around, her eyes searching for what she'd just seen. And then, as her gaze passed over the mirror maze, she found it.

Out of the jumble of mirrors, a zillion reflections of Charlotte's face glared at her.

Nancy bought a ticket, and stepped inside the maze. Charlotte's reflection had disappeared, but Nancy hadn't seen her leave. She had to still be inside.

Nancy quickly hit a dead end. With her own reflection staring at her from all sides, she tried a passage to the right. Once more, her own blue eyes gazed back at her from the mirror blocking her way. She turned around, ready to try another path.

Suddenly Charlotte's face filled every mirror in sight. Nancy whipped around. Charlotte's reflections laughed, teasing Nancy, delighted by her confusion. *Which was the real person?* Nancy wondered, frustrated.

Nancy turned down a passage to her left and caught a glimpse of Charlotte's back in the mirrors ahead. *Just let me out of here!* Nancy thought. *What if Charlotte escapes while I'm stuck in this crazy maze?* But in every passage she took, Nancy was a prisoner of her own reflection. Until she turned another corner. . . .

Just three feet away from Nancy, the real Charlotte froze. She was trapped. Thanks to the mirrors around them, Nancy anticipated Charlotte's next move. As Charlotte reached into her pocket, Nancy threw up her hands to shield her face.

Charlotte whipped out a Discman. She swung it against the walls, shattering their reflections. Shards of glass rained over Nancy's hands and arms.

16

The Mystery Team

Once all the glass had fallen, Charlotte shoved Nancy aside and ran down the passage. Gingerly, Nancy straightened and shook herself off. Glass clinked to the floor. Peering into an unbroken mirror, Nancy checked to see if she was okay. Other than a few minor cuts on her hands and arms from shielding her head, she was unharmed. With one more shake of her T-shirt just in case, Nancy took off after Charlotte, glass crunching underfoot.

There were more dead ends at every turn. By the time Nancy found her way out of the maze, she'd already lost a few minutes.

After warning the attendant about the broken glass, Nancy scanned the area for Charlotte, *Don't tell me I've lost her after all this*, she thought.

Nancy then noticed a slim blond figure moving quickly through the crowd. Charlotte! Nancy raced after her. The moment Charlotte noticed Nancy gaining on her, she broke into a run. But a huge ride was in her way: the bumper cars.

Instead of avoiding it, Charlotte headed right for the attraction. She leaped over the rail, into the middle of the crashing cars.

Nancy didn't flinch. She hurtled over the rail after Charlotte and caught up to her just as a car bore down on them.

"Hey!" the operator yelled. "What are you two doing? Get out of there!" He flipped a switch, and the cars whined to a halt.

Charlotte ran toward the far side of the platform, her loafers slipping on the smooth metal surface. She skidded for a moment, then fell. Desperately, she scrambled up, clutching a bumper car for support.

Wearing sneakers, Nancy kept her grip on the platform. Without slipping once, she caught up to Charlotte, and tackled her to the floor.

"Get off me!" Charlotte yelled. "I'll have you arrested for assault!"

"Okay, just as long as you also tell the police you attacked me with that glass?" Nancy retorted, pinning Charlotte in a judo hold.

"That was just . . . an unfortunate accident," Charlotte growled. Her body tensed, as if a huge fury was raging inside her. But suddenly, her shoulders sagged. Nancy could tell that she had given up.

Charlotte took a deep breath before speaking. "Lighten up on my shoulders, Nancy—and I'll tell you the whole truth."

The ride operator approached them. A hostile look flashed in his eyes. "Didn't you two hear me? Get out of here, now. I'm calling the police."

"Please call them right away," Nancy said as she loosened her grip on Charlotte's shoulders. "Ask for Chief McGinnis or Officer Rivken. Tell them Nancy Drew caught the person we've been looking for— the one who's been bothering Green Spring."

The man instantly calmed down. "Yeah—sure thing." After announcing to the bumper car passengers that the ride was temporarily closed, he hurried off.

"Okay, Charlotte," Nancy said. "You promised to tell me the truth. What was in that envelope you handed to James Fenwick?"

"Cash," Charlotte said bluntly.

"For what?"

"I gave him money to sabotage Green Spring," Charlotte said. She turned her face abruptly as a tear slid down her cheek. "His loyalty to it was easy to sway. His brother was at a rival camp; I think he'd been turned down by Mrs. Rogers last year because she didn't have room." More tears ran down her cheeks, and she angrily wiped them away. "He was a good worker for a while. He did most of the pranks at the camp, but he got cold feet at the rally. He wanted Reed to compete legitimately. So I had to do the work here myself," she complained.

"You set off that firecracker, and stole Tarzan?" Nancy asked.

"And misdirected the flag," Charlotte said. "The monkey was a pain in the neck. He bit me on the arm when I took him from his pen. I had to coax him into the barrel with a banana. I'm amazed *that* part of my plan worked—but it did," she added smugly.

"You said James did the stuff at Green Spring? Did he think of it all himself?" Nancy asked.

"Everything was my idea," she replied, shaking her head. "He just did what I asked."

"Do you know how Josh Bryant's letter opener ended up on the tack room floor at the camp?" Nancy asked.

"I wondered where I'd left that," Charlotte said. "Wrecking the saddle was the only thing I actually did at Green Spring. James was feeling bad about all the problems he'd been causing, so he went on strike for a day. I sneaked in with Josh's opener and slashed up the saddle."

"Where'd you get the opener?" Nancy asked.

"I lifted it from Josh's party a few months ago," Charlotte replied. "My plan to close Green Spring was already swimming around in my head. The opener was a way to throw suspicion onto Josh. But I have to admit, Nancy, you were too smart for me." Charlotte paused, her lip trembling.

Nancy continued with her line of questioning. "Are you upset because your plan didn't work?"

"I'm upset because I caused so much trouble," Charlotte replied.

Nancy wasn't sure whether Charlotte was sincere. "Well, why did you want to hurt Green Spring?" Nancy asked. "What did you have to gain? Your mother and Mrs. Rogers were best friends—so why shut it down?"

Charlotte's eyes snapped with anger. "That's just it," she declared. "Their friendship hurt me!"

"How?"

"My late mother left half her money in trust to Green Spring," Charlotte said bitterly, "because she and Madeline Rogers were best friends. Madeline wanted to start a scholarship program that would give aid to kids who needed it, and my mother thought that was a fine idea."

"You're angry at Mrs. Rogers because she got half your mom's money," Nancy said, trying to make sense of Charlotte's words, "so you've been attacking Green Spring for revenge?"

"Revenge is stupid," Charlotte replied. "What's the point of crying over spilled milk? I did this for money."

"Money? How would you get money by closing down Green Spring?" Nancy asked.

"Because my mother's will says that if Green Spring shuts down, the money reverts to me so I can set up a similar camp—one with a scholarship program," Charlotte explained.

Nancy was surprised. Charlotte was interested in needy children who want to ride?

"You did all these things so you could get enough money to set up a similar camp?" Nancy asked.

"No way!" Charlotte retorted. "I'm not interested in hanging out with bratty kids and their horses. In my mother's will, there's no provision for what would happen to the money if my camp program shut down. So I planned to create a second-rate program that would close after a year. Then I could do whatever I wanted with the money. I could quit my job at the store and take off for Hawaii."

"If you're unhappy with your job, there are plenty of legal ways to earn money," Nancy said reasonably. "You don't have to endanger teenagers and animals in some elaborate plot to shut down a riding camp. And why did you buy Equestrian Outfitters if you don't like working there?"

"My mother owned that store," Charlotte explained, "so I got stuck with it, instead of with the other half of her cash. That money should have been mine." Charlotte's sniffling became a sudden flood of tears. "I'm sorry, Nancy," she murmured. "I really am sorry. Yes, the money should have been mine, but I didn't mean to hurt anyone. I didn't actually *hurt* anyone—did I?"

"People were really scared," Nancy said. "A girl's arm was bruised when she slipped by the pool, a counselor got poison ivy, and property was ruined. It's lucky that you *didn't* hurt anyone very badly."

Charlotte looked at her with mournful eyes. "I missed my mother so much after she died." She paused for a moment. "I thought I deserved all her money."

Nancy was tempted to tell Charlotte that her mother had died, too, but that didn't make her feel entitled to things that weren't hers. She realized, though, Charlotte's mind had broken a little with grief. *There's no way this woman is thinking logically*, Nancy mused. *Maybe with time—and medical help—Charlotte one day will be cured.*

At that moment, Officer Rivken appeared and took charge of Charlotte. Nancy explained that James was also involved. They could probably find him back at the stables.

When the squad car dropped Nancy off outside Green Spring's tack room, James was in the doorway, chatting with Elsa, George, Cordelia, and Mrs. Rogers. His face paled when he saw Charlotte inside the squad car, and Nancy and Officer Rivken climbing out. The rest of the astonished pony club team gathered around as Nancy took James aside and started to question him.

She quickly told him Charlotte's story. His gaze flickered to Charlotte sobbing away in the backseat. "She told you the truth, Nancy," James said tentatively. "She paid me generously to do all that stuff at camp. I even swiped Clare's olive oil to pour by the pool. When I overheard Mrs. Rogers hiring you, I got worried. I followed you home and soaped your window, hoping to scare you off. But I guess it didn't work."

Mrs. Rogers stared at him. "You should be ashamed of yourself, James Fenwick. You could have killed someone! All those pranks were really dangerous. Did you only think of how much you were getting paid?"

James hung his head in shame. "I'm sorry. What I did was greedy, and stupid, and very wrong. But I wised up by the time the rally came, and I refused to work for Charlotte anymore. She paid me today for the things I did at Green Spring," he added, removing the envelope from his jeans pocket. "Here, Mrs. Rogers. Take this money and use it for your scholarships."

"I can't believe you would do those awful things, James," Elsa said. "I mean, what kind of example are you setting for Reed—and for our pony club?"

James's face reddened. "I never meant to set a bad example. I thought at the time that I needed the money, but it really wasn't worth it. I'm sorry, everyone," he added, scanning the stunned faces of the Green Spring riders, "and please, Mrs. Rogers, tell Reed I'm sorry too." James got into the backseat of Officer Rivken's car with Charlotte, and the car drove off.

Everyone on the team looked at one another in silent shock. Then Katie took a deep breath and said, "It's strange to think that James did all that stuff— but at least Green Spring is safe again."

The mood around the stable remained somber, but relieved. The competition was just ending. As soon as the stadium jumping finished, tension mounted. The final results would be announced at any moment!

Suddenly, the loudspeaker blared, "All teams please assemble on horseback outside the grandstand for the parade of winners!"

Fifteen minutes later, the six teams were grouped on the track in front of the grandstand. Elsa, George, Nancy, Bess, and Mrs. Rogers waited tensely on the sidelines. A rally official came forward with a large silver trophy and blue ribbons. He cleared his throat and announced, "And the winner is: Green Spring!"

Gasps of joy erupted as the teammates gave one

another the thumbs-up sign. Cordelia accepted the trophy on behalf of the team. Everyone cheered as the official pinned ribbons on each horse's bridle, and Cordelia called the counselors and Mrs. Rogers out to join them.

"Nancy, I want to thank you on behalf of the team for your great detective work," Cordelia said, smiling. "And I want to thank Mrs. Rogers for her wonderful pony club, Green Spring, which is just so awesome. Now that the mystery is solved, the camp and its scholarships can keep going strong." She held up the trophy. "Everyone, look out! Green Spring rules!"

Mrs. Rogers beamed. "Hooray! Thanks for your great work, kids, and yes—many, many thanks to Nancy for all her help."

"I want to thank my own winning rally team of mystery-busters," Nancy said, glancing at her two best friends. "Bess and George!"

"Oooh . . . does that mean we go to the *mystery* nationals?" George joked.

"Well, if there's a mystery, we always rally around," Bess said, with her trademark smile.

Nancy Drew® on CD-ROM!

Danger and Intrigue Await You in Five Fully Interactive 3-D Mystery Games!

Secrets Can Kill
Read between the lines as supersleuth Nancy Drew to find a killer!

Stay Tuned for Danger
Go undercover to save daytime TV's biggest star from the danger lurking in the wings.

Message in a Haunted Mansion
Discover who—or what—is behind the mysterious accidents in a house full of secrets.

Treasure in the Royal Tower
Follow ancient clues to expose a castle's legendary secret.

The Final Scene
Search a darkened movie theater to free a hostage from her captor's dangerous plot.

For Ages 10 and Up

EVERYONE
E
CONTENT RATED BY ESRB

Visit **www.herinteractive.com** for a Sneak Preview!

Order Now!
www.herinteractive.com
or call 1-800-561-0908

WINDOWS 95/98/2000/ME/XP

www.dreamcatchergames.com

"For Girls Who Aren't Afraid of a Mouse"